A lonely young man, a temporary job. A befuddled old woman living in the house where she was born. Two characters off-balance moment to moment, one vigilant, both lost. Day after day after day, nothing changes. She will not get better. Yet this exquisitely detailed narrative of caretaking and commitment is also a nuanced meditation on the nature of happiness. When will her life come to an end? When will his begin? *Birds of Massachusetts* is a profoundly moving inquiry into what it is to be in the world. **—Michelle Carter**

A magnificent investigation of memory, *Birds of Massachusetts* is a quiet storm of tenderness. Gorgeously written and tragic, we delve into the corners of memory as a young man cares for a terminally ill older woman dealing with dementia. A story about finding meaning in the mundane and everydayness, the objects and books around the house bloom to life. It is in the soft repetition of routines that our protagonist finds comfort. At the very core, it is a story about the solace of connection, and the grand impact of small gestures. **—Juliana Delgado Lopera, judge for the 2019 Clark-Gross Award in the Novel**

This book is so beautifully realized that describing it might cause it to fly away. But I will reveal that it has two characters, an elderly woman suffering from Alzheimer's and the young man who takes her to lunch every day. We never learn their names, but we get to know them intimately. Because of her memory loss, each day they must begin their acquaintance fresh, like the movie *Groundhog Day*. The young man brings a book to read to her, but she quickly falls asleep at the kitchen table, surrounded by photos from her vibrant earlier life. Every day is the same, and this circularity has an almost choral beauty. She never remembers him, but she finds him to be wonderful. The wind blows, and the trees break into applause. The young man thinks as she sleeps: "I am delicate even turning the page because I'm afraid that any movement will come with sound—the chair crying out through your memory—waking you. So I am still. I am still. I am still in this chair." Though the story's pattern is sameness, it is as deep as life and as bold as a song by Johnny Cash. —**Paul Hoover**

I love this little book, this spare, flickering dual portrait of unlikely companions, one of whom is paid to keep the other company and required to re-establish himself daily, as her memory is damaged. There is uncanny drama in this record of their repeated days, as his inhibition and her sociability are in ever-renewed confrontation. With a deliberately limited palette that showcases his resourcefulness, and a real allergy to pretensions of any kind, Steven Kennedy creates an unlabored pathos that reminds me of Emmanuel Bove. And this modestly ingenious experiment in the poetics of the reset joins other classics in the tradition: James Lord's *A Giacometti Portrait*, Renee Gladman's *Calamities*, and *Malone Dies*, by Samuel Beckett. As a quiet evocation of senescence and awakening, its originality is unforgettable. —**Brian Blanchfield**

Birds of Massachusetts

In memory of Michael Rubin, Fourteen Hills Press annually publishes a book of exceptional accomplishment by a student or recent graduate. Each book is selected through an open competition by an independent judge.

The 2020 Michael Rubin Book Award was judged by Brian Blanchfield.

Fourteen Hills Press
San Francisco, CA
ISBN: 978-1-889292-80-9
Printed in the United States of America.

Library of Congress Control Number: 2020919021

Cover art by Laura Donworth.
Author photo by Stuart Ballew.

Cover design by Aleesha Lange.
Typesetting by Rachel Huefner.

Birds of Massachusetts

Steven Kennedy

Winner of the 2020 Michael Rubin Book Award

Fourteen Hills ⸝ San Francisco State University

To my grandparents: Vince & Adeline Barbaria, Robert
& Donna Kennedy

To Laura

To M. B. S. , *in memory*

I.

Ernest Hemingway's 'A Day's Wait'

THE STORY BEFORE 'A Natural History of the Dead' in *The Short Stories* by Ernest Hemingway is 'A Day's Wait.' I read this story to myself while you sleep.

The sun is warm through the window and though it is cold outside, I am sweating just sitting there in the chair at the kitchen table, so I stand up and quietly take off my sweater. I do not want to wake you.

The hedge below the window is thinning. The trees that line the yard are drying out, changing color, and losing their leaves. In the summer, the view of the harbor is blocked by their leaf-laden branches but now that they are emptying, I can see through them, all the way down to the lighthouse past the rocky neck in town to Granite Pier, pointing out from the bottom of the hill your house sits on.

You are snoring. I fold my sweater and hang it over the back of my chair where I had placed my coat earlier. I had come in up the long hallway, the same as always. I had come into the kitchen and sat down across the table from you, the same as always. I said good morning and you smiled at me, same as always, and I could tell that you didn't know I was coming. I could tell by the way your eyes changed shapes as they moved over my face that you did not remember me. But you never remember me—this morning is the same as always.

The way your eyes change shapes remind me of water.

And when I had come in earlier and sat down in the chair across the table from you, your husband started gathering his things.

Where are you going? you asked.

To run some errands. And he looked at me. I'll be back at 1:15.

I nodded and he said goodbye to you and you

turned away and told him that you would not be saying goodbye because husbands shouldn't leave their wives. You asked me if I felt the same way and I said yes but he would be back soon and he would not be gone for long. You shook your head and said again that you would not be saying goodbye and you put your head down on the table so your skirt of gray hair fell over your face and I could no longer see it. Your husband smiled at me and went down the stairs to the garage.

The story 'A Day's Wait' is short and that is why I picked it. I read it while you sleep, the hump of your shoulder lifting unevenly with each breath.

You mumble something into the table. You say something like yes...oh yes those are lovely, aren't they?

I glance up from the book but do not respond. You talk in your sleep often. It is usually nonsense. You often say Wonderful! or, Goodness no!

Once you said: A lot of birds flying around this morning. I can see their shadows—which I wrote down and worked out and is actually a haiku.

I finish the story, look up and your head is still on the table. I check the time. We have more than an hour before I take you into town for lunch where we always go to the same cafe. The staff all know you. They know you are sick and I am there to help you. The owner and his wife greet us as we come in. The waitress hugs you as I fold up your walker and leave it outside. Hi darling! She says. What is it today? The usual? You laugh and say, The usual sounds delicious...but what is it? She smiles, glances at me as I remind you that you always order a grilled cheese with bacon and a coffee. You purse your lips and narrow your eyes. Sounds delicious. I'll have that, you say as you shuffle your way to our table in the back with its plastic chairs and plastic tablecloth that looks out on the harbor.

But it is still early and you are asleep. There is nothing else to do so I start the Hemingway story over again. It is only three pages and it'd be nice to read it again, to really understand it.

'A Day's Wait' is about a boy who is sick with a temperature of one hundred and two. The doctor says he has the flu and prescribes him some medicine to take. The boy's father reads to the boy in bed but he is not listening to the story. He sits there and does not sleep, which would be normal, but the way the boy stares at the foot of his bed is very strange. The father closes the book and suggests the boy sleeps but the boy shakes him off. "You don't have to stay in here with me, Papa, if it bothers you," the boy says and the father says it does not bother him. The boy then clarifies "No, I mean, you don't have to stay if it's going to bother you." The father thinks this is an odd thing to say but does not give it more thought. When it is time, he gives the boy his medicine and decides to go out to get some air.

Again, you talk in your sleep, mumbling something about how dinner is on the table and it's nice to sit down as a family every now and then.

I do not look up. You are not talking to me.

The father takes his dog and goes hunting. He shoots some quail but misses more than he kills because it is cold and icy out and he does not have good footing, which is important when it comes to marksmanship. When the father returns to the house, the boy has refused to let anyone else enter his room. He did not want anybody to catch what he had and told them to stay away. The father goes into the room and the boy does not look better. He is still looking strangely at the foot of his bed. The father takes his temperature and the boy is concerned. He overheard the doctor and knows his temperature is at one hundred and two. The father assures him that there is nothing to worry about. He continues the story he was reading earlier but again, the boy does not listen. He asks his father "About how long will it be before I die?" The father thinks this is a ridiculous question and ignores it, but the boy persists and says that at his school in France he had heard that a person can't live with a temperature past forty-four. In that moment, at the boy's bedside, the father understands that his son is, and was, preparing to die. The line goes "He had been waiting to die all day, ever since nine o'clock in the morning" and the father reassures him that one hundred and two and forty-four is the difference between miles and kilometers and the boy would be fine. The boy understands and slowly relaxes. The next day he is without symptoms and the story ends saying that the boy was back to normal and "cried very easily at little things that were of no importance."

Your kitchen has become hotter. I am still sweating and I wish I could take off another layer. You coo and shift your weight in your chair. I do not know how you sleep like that: head flat on the table, back bent at the hip, leaning in from your chair.

You shift in your chair, mumble, then, you wake. Your eyes are wet. You sit up and brush the hair from your face. You look at me and your pupils are so small they appear pointed. You fold your hands on your lap and lean forward, sighing heavily.

Oh, it's warm in here.
Yes it is.
Making me tired.
Yes.
You laugh into the table.
So warm in here.
Yes.

I'm exhausted.

I nod.

Why don't you read me something while I just put my head down.

You sigh again as if you had just been relieved of a heavy bag.

Read me something short from that book you got.

Ok, I say.

I turn the page back to the beginning and start to read.

This story is called 'A Day's Wait' by Ernest Hemingway.

Oh how lovely, you say, chuckling into the table.

I get to the part where the father notices his boy is not listening to the book he is reading when I notice you are not listening to the book I am reading. You are asleep again. The hump of your shoulder rising and falling and rising again. The morning is as long as the heat. There is still plenty of time before we head into town, plenty of time to kill, so I continue on, reading the story to myself as you mumble into the table something from your dreams.

In the mornings, I knock on the front door.

It is always open. Your husband cracks it open so I can let myself in. I do not need to knock, but I knock anyway because I want you to know that I am here. I knock on the front door because I want you to hear that someone is here and someone is coming.

In the mornings, I push open the door and step into your home. I say hello. I say it, then I sing it. I try to sound happy when I sing my *hell-o*. I read somewhere that if I am happy, it will help you to be happy. I read somewhere that people with your sickness remember emotions rather than names. Or, I should say that they remember emotions better than names. The people with your sickness latch on to how people make them feel. I do not know if that is true for you, but I still sing my *hell-o*. I sing my *hell-o* and hope you feel happy because of my light, birdsong tone as you hear the knock on the front door and wonder who is here so early in the morning.

I enter your house. I sing my *hell-o*. I sing to remind myself that I should be happy.

It is hard sometimes, coming into your house, knowing that I will not be known, knowing that the coming hours will be the same hours I've spent with you for however many days it's been since I've been coming to you.

I wipe my feet on the mat and step into the long hallway that runs the length of the house from the front door to the kitchen where you and your husband sit each morning. There you are at the table, watching television, eating breakfast, waiting for me. But you do not know you are waiting. You do not know that I am coming. You hear a knock on the front door. You hear me sing my *hell-o* and you turn to your husband and ask who is that? Who is that at the door? Your husband starts to get up, he puts his hand on your shoulder to make you feel okay and for support as he gets up from his chair. He has to get ready to go. He tells you who it is, telling you that I come every morning while he is out at work or running errands. This is news to you. You do not remember me but you understand that your husband is going. He is gathering his things. You understand, suddenly, that this is what is happening on this morning that was like every other morning before there was a knock at the door, you heard someone sing hell-o, and your husband got up to go.

I am walking slow up the long hallway in your home.

Why do you need to leave? Why does someone need to come and stay with me in my own house? I hear you ask these questions. I am getting deeper into your home, walking slow, slower, hearing you not understand as your husband gets up from the table to greet me, to get ready to go. He tells you that this is how it's been for awhile now. He tells you that I come in the mornings, then take you into town to get lunch and that's how it has been for months now, but what are months to you? What is a year? Or even a day? You do not remember any of this and then you hear a knock on your door and everything changes.

I try to make my steps soft. I walk slow. I don't want to intrude.

You have lived here your whole life—I see this walking the long hallway, getting deeper into your house, this home that you've lived in for however many years your life has become.

I see the picture of you as a girl in the yard. It looks like your first day of school. Your dress is pleated and firm, your shoes are white and your socks are pulled up. There is the front door I just walked through.

Even in black and white, your eyes are the same.

I see the picture of you and your sister sitting on a sled, waiting to ride the slope of the hill your house is built on.

Your eyes are the same even in snow.

I see the picture of you holding a newborn wrapped in a blue blanket. I see you and your husband kneeling at the altar.

I am getting deeper into your home and I feel the panic of being somewhere I should not be. I tell myself that I answered an ad. I am supposed to be here. This is my job. I parked in the driveway as I've done for months now. I knocked on the door at the time that was expected of me.

I hear you asking why.

Why is this happening?

I am getting deeper into your home and on the walls: a college diploma, a painting of a shipwreck, children in bathing suits playing with a garden hose, an infant's baptism, a photograph of a dog with its tongue out. The dog stands over a stretch of chewed, knotted rope, its chocolate brown coat lit by the sun. It was summer then—I have seen a summer here. I expand the image in my head. Beyond the edges of the photograph is the hedge full of flickering wings. Tiny birds flitting in and out of the twigs and leaves, poking their heads out and moving from branch to feeder to branch to the stone bath. In the summer, in this photograph of the dog, the trees lining the yard are heavy with leaves. After rain, the bark is soaked dark and the leaves are lanterns of gelatinous green.

This is what you see each morning. Nothing about this has changed. Fall becomes winter. Winter becomes spring and the spring is short here—it turns quickly into summer.

You have lived here your whole life. Each morning, you go out to sit at the kitchen table and look out the window. You see the dog. You see your two children in the sprinklers. You see them throwing a baseball. You see your husband tossing the hose to the ground, gathering the apples from the orchard. You see the neighbor on her knees behind the low stone wall. You see your sister in her swimsuit and she is calling for you to come down and hurry, she is heading to the quarry and doesn't want to wait much longer.

But now it is different—you heard a knock on the door. There was a song. Something has changed yet nothing has changed. You do not understand, but you look up at me when I finally turn the corner from the hallway into the kitchen.

Hell-o, I sing and you look up at me and smile.

Good morning, you say, and your eyes move over me. Your husband mutes the TV. I sit down across from you.

I sit in the same chair each morning. I walk into the kitchen and sit in the chair across the table from you. The chair is small and old. It is wooden with a rounded frame and legs and a flat back. Its seat is made of woven straw with a red cushion placed on top to make it more comfortable. It is more comfortable, but not comfortable.

I sit in the chair and when I sit down, the chair's joints crackle like a fire. They negotiate my weight. When I move my leg, draping one knee over the other, the joints squeal. I lean forward and the chair whines. The chair is small and old and probably meant for a child. I can see you sitting in it as a kid. Feet hanging, swinging, making it squeak as you sit at the dinner table eating, not eating, moving your food around. Your cheeks are full like a squirrel's. There is not a wrinkle on your face and your hair is pulled to either side of your head and curling out like pom-poms from behind your ears. You are sitting in this chair, swinging your legs under the table trying to make the joints crackle like a fire. Your eyes are the same as they are now: sharp and mischievous. Your father and mother ignore you, knowing that you are making the racket on purpose. Your sister is copying you, trying to copy you— she is younger than you and smaller than you and that will always be the case. You have always reminded her of that. She has her own chair and I imagine it is the same as yours as mine.

I come to your house and sit in the same chair across the table from you.

I sit and I am so quiet sitting there, you get bored and laugh.

I'm just going to put my head down, you say. Let me know if anything interesting is happening.

I say ok and watch as you lay your head down to rest on the table. When you close your eyes, I am relieved. I feel like I can relax. I settle in, pick up a book, and think about nothing. I cross one leg over the other to get comfortable and the chair sounds. The wicker whines under the strain. The chair's joints crackle like a fire and you hear it in your rest. You recognize the sound and you know that legs are swinging, children are getting restless. I am sure both of your kids sat in this chair when they were younger. This chair and another, its sibling around here somewhere— in storage in another room. Two chairs for you and your sister. Two for your two boys. They sat at the table eating dinner, pushing their dinner around, swinging their legs under the table so their chairs would make sound. They would glance at each other, they would glance at you and your husband, trying to keep their faces straight as they wiggled and kicked their hips and legs under the table. They pinch their lips to keep themselves from laughing. You do not get annoyed. Small devils. Your husband gets annoyed. He rolls his eyes and tries to ignore it, keeps his head down on his dinner. The sound of the chair, the joints and the wicker and the wood and you look up and ask

How's it going over there?

I glance up from my book. Your head is tilted up and I can barely make out your eyes. You're half asleep. I hear the water cracking in your throat.

Again: How's it going over there?

and your children freeze, go silent. They look up at you and hang there, frozen, in your eyes. They can never tell if you are serious or not, angry or not, they can never tell if you are on the verge of reprimand or laughter—they try to find it in your eyes but they can never be sure.

They do not have your eyes and I do not have your eyes either.

You mumble something and we hang in a moment at the end of your eyes.

But your head lowers. You are sleeping again. The hump of your shoulder swells and falls with each ragged, uneven snore. I settle into this chair, into this book, across the table from you. I try not to move my head or my legs, I am delicate even turning the page because I'm afraid that any movement will come with a sound—the chair crying out through your memory—waking you.

So I am still. I am still. I am still in this chair. You are sleeping with your head on the table and your hair skirting down from the blue line of skin at the top of your head. Your hair covers your face where your eyes are. They are closed now and hidden. You are asleep and I do not want to wake you.

We are not related you and I. None of your blood is in me. I am here in your kitchen, across the table from you, writing to you reading to you talking to you, because I answered an ad in the newspaper. Your husband still goes to work in the mornings, he needed someone to look after you while he was away at the office and running errands. I get paid to be here with you. I would not be here if that was not the case.

You can no longer be on your own, though you say otherwise. You are too weak and sick. Your balance is not good. You had a stroke recently, it was your second in as many years. Your memory is going. When we drive into town and someone recognizes you on the street and they approach us and ask how you are doing and how your children are doing, you laugh and say fine fine everything's fine and you take their hand in yours and say to them I am so embarrassed but remind me who you are again. They are polite and whisper their name to you like it is the next line of a play and you are on stage and you say oh yes of course and laugh and repeat their name aloud for the audience to hear. They nod and turn to me and say you must be the grandson and I say oh no I'm just a friend going out to lunch, or oh no I'm just the driver, and they smile and understand because it is a small town—you have lived here a long time—and they know that you are not doing well. You have dementia, Alzheimer's, I think, I am not sure. You do not know what you have. You say your memory is not so good and chuckle because you are getting old. I couldn't even tell you how old I am, you say.

Your husband does not tell me what is specifically wrong with your body and mind and I do not ask. He covers the assorted orange pill bottles at the middle of the table with a white tea towel when I walk in each morning. When he leaves, I could lift the towel and examine the labels, write down the names of the drugs and their dosages you take each day on a piece of paper and look them up when I am home but I do not and will not.

You are old and sick. I do not need to know that blood is clotting in your brain or neurons are dying and synaptic signaling is decreasing between cells to understand that. When I walk into your kitchen each morning you do not remember me. I sit down across the table from you and I see your mind working behind your eyes, trying to connect the world you see in front of you with the world you had laid out in your mind. I do not need to know that your brain is experiencing severe tissue loss and physically shrinking to understand that your mind is now deeper and more mysterious than ever and when you peel back your lips painted wet with lipstick and say to me, remind me who you are again, you are asking for the next line.

Remind me your name again.

It is my job to whisper back my name.

I whisper back my name.

I feel compelled to reassure you that I have never changed it. I have never told you a different name, a made-up one. I've never done that. The fact that I'm saying that I'm sure makes it sound like I have changed it before, but I never have, I promise you. I could've changed it—I don't know why I would've—but you could've asked for my name one morning and I could've said anything. Any name, that could've been me for the day.

I could say any name, but I never have.

I promise you.

I also think that we've been together long enough that you would know if I lied to you. You couldn't tell me my real name off the top of your head but you would know if I changed it. I don't know how but you would know. You would sense something was off. I would lie to you and you would say nothing. You would mouth the name. You would whisper it again as you bobbed your head along with each of its syllables, feeling the shape of it with your lips, something about it not being right.

I'm not a good liar either. I would mess it up somehow by some weird tick or uneasy smirk, adjusting my weight sitting in the chair across the table from you.

Even if I was a good liar, I'm too afraid to try anyway.

I think it's your eyes—I am afraid of your eyes. They are beautiful.

Eyes are windows to the soul, looking glasses, camera shutters, pools, black holes, and possessors. All of this has been said about eyes. I don't really know what all that means but I can say it feels true about your eyes too.

When I look at you and you look at me with those eyes I become afraid because they are penetrating while being impenetrable. I am pinned by them, under a microscope with nowhere to go, nothing to do, but be seen.

You see me and yet, I feel like I can't see you.

You say, remind me your name again? And I think to change it but I don't. I look into your eyes and they are so beautiful and flat and I lean forward over the table between us and whisper to you my name. You sit up and say the name aloud and nod because it is true.

You pick up your head and your face is small with pinched lips and focused eyes. They are set, looking at me—they don't move. And then, all of sudden, you shiver and they flinch. You pull your hair back and your expression slackens. A release, like a sigh. You laugh and drop your head.

I thought you were my husband, you say.

Oh no. Just me.

I sit up in my chair so you can see that it is just me.

Did I tell you he took me dancing last night?

That sounds fun.

It was at a place in town, overlooking the water.

Sounds nice.

Oh, very nice.

You tell me that you had fish and wine.

You tell me it was warm so you sat on the deck under the string lights that were faint enough to see past them to the stars and moon. You could hear the water too, lapping under the deck. You tell me the restaurant had a little music group out there playing old stand-bys, the classics from the radio when you were a kid. You knew the words and sang. You ate and danced and ate and danced.

Sounds very nice.

You'll have to go sometime. You can take someone—it is very romantic out on the deck.

Sounds very nice, I say again.

It was in town. Right on the water. The restaurant had a deck and a band was playing. We were eating and then, when the band started to play a song we liked, we popped right up and started to dance, just like that. Our food was still in our mouths! Oh, it was wonderful. It was like when we were first married! Oh it was wonderful.

You sigh into the table. I look at you—your closed eyes flinch and flicker like you are playing a film across the inside of your eyelids.

For a moment I can see you in it: this memory of dancing with your husband; this memory of night with stars out and black water, flecked yellow and silver stretching out beyond you. The tisk of the drum beat. The rain of piano keys. Wine and fish. I can hear the dull chime of rigging and lines off nearby masts, the silverware on dishware, the heels and laughter. I see you and it is you now and you then—a strange mix of the You in front of me and the You I have seen in the photographs around the house. Young and old—it is You. I see you but you are far off, a stranger across the deck, half obscured by heads and lifting arms, tilting wine glasses and waiters in aprons taking orders and laying out dishes. There is this great busyness between us. The tisk of the drum beat. The rain of piano keys. Wine and fish. The dull chime of rigging and silverware. Limbs and lives between us. You and your husband turn and turn. I can't see your face—your hair wisps as you turn. You and your husband lean in and say something to each other I can not hear.

Everything is turning and rolling on...and now all of it is gone.

You'll have to go sometime, you say. You can take someone—it is very romantic out on the deck.

Sounds very nice, I say again.

You close your eyes tight and I can see that you are replaying the memory again in your head as it drops to the table.

You settle into it: your sleep and dreams.

And of course, last night was cold. The first cold night of the year. A cold you feel rage against your throat as you breathe it in, pushing down the air.

You did not go out dancing—I know this.

I sit back in my chair. It is so warm in your kitchen

with the sun out and radiating through the glass. The sky is clear and unbroken. It looks like it could be the first day of spring, but I know it is not.

I know, out there, fall is on us. Everything cold-bit.

And what did I do last night?

I hear the wind barreling past my window. The papered page. My eyes out of focus on the papered page, listening to the wind. Feet under the pillow on my couch, thinking about the thermostat. Resisting the urge to turn on the heat, hunkering down into the couch, an aluminum beer.

I am in my basement room. My copy of *Moby Dick* split open and face down on my stomach. I am not reading it, but listening to the wind against the window in my basement room. It is there high on the adjacent wall above my desk. The pane is painted black with night—it gets dark early now. If it was summer, it would still be light out, and even though my room is in the basement and the window is level to the ground looking out to the woods behind the house, I could still read by the natural light coming through the glass. In the summer, I was in sync with this light. The sun would go down at just the right time as I'd start to tire. My room would get dark and my eyes would get heavy. I would close my book, my head would go to the pillow and my room would be black.

It was so hot then.

It feels impossible that it was ever, or could ever be, that hot now that summer is over and we are into autumn and it is so cold at night.

It was damp then too. My towel in the bathroom never dried. It'd get so musty down here. I'd hang it on the laundry line outside but that rarely did the trick either. A couple of times I had forgotten about it outside on the line and it got rained on. Rain came fast in the summer.

The window in my room would always be open then too. The sound of birds and peepers and insects would come in from the woods and sift through the black mesh screen and fill the room with a constant hum. The sound roughed up the air. It was textured and hot with unseen bodies colliding and shells being shucked and wood being chewed. I loved the sound of leather feathers and wind sigh and wood crack and like I said before, wood being chewed.

It feels so long ago it is almost as if it didn't happen. It feels impossible—summer and its heat—sitting here on my couch in the foxing lamp light.

I cover my legs in a blanket and bury my feet under a pillow. I take a sip of beer. I pick up *Moby Dick* from my stomach and read the first line and the first line goes Call me Ishmael.

Call me Ishmael, it goes and then the words continue on, but I stop to sneeze. The book has that musty smell flattened into its binding—I have not opened it in a long time. The pages are yellow and spotting. I hold the book in front of me and sneeze into it.

The tenants' laundry machine runs in the other room. The machine vibrates as it spins, tapping against the wall by my head. The plaster so thin the smell of lemon detergent breaks through it. The machine clucks against the wall like water against a boat's hull. I am berthed below deck, halfway underwater.

Call me Ishmael.

I lay the book down again.

I feel certain sitting on this couch. It is my couch in my room. The wind goes outside the window and the laundry machine runs on the other side of the wall and I am here. Safe. I am wrapped up, protected and removed from their sounds knocking against my ears, their chill and unfamiliarity. I do not need to address them. I am not responsible for their noise. I have bowled out a neat and dry space for myself here in this basement room against the unfathomable black of the ocean.

I sip my beer and think about how you talk from your dreams. It is terrifying at first, how it is spontaneous and frank and comes from nowhere, but I remind myself that you are not talking to me. I remind myself to make that table between us in your kitchen a window, or a plaster wall, so I can just sit and listen without having to worry about what you say on the other side of it.

No expectations. No need to respond, to reach out with words into that space between us and attempt a bridge. My mind to yours. Maybe one morning, I'll just mirror you when you sleep. I'll lay my head down and we'll use the table to amplify and muddy and cool all the sounds between us. We'll both just talk directly from our memories.

The reading light casts a dim veil over the rest of my room. There is my bed—just a mattress on the floor. There is my desk under the window with some notebooks and papers and some books stacked on it. Its chair is there too, pulled out slightly and piled with clothes waiting to be folded and clothes already worn. Yesterday's pants hang their legs over the wooden back—I will probably wear these tomorrow too. There are my books, pushed against the wall in four columns. No shelf. No bookcase. They have been there since I moved here and unboxed them. They went from boxes in my car to wonky stacks in my room. Some of them I have read and loved and held onto and lugged across the country and some of them I have bought and never read but held and hold onto still because I should read them, I know I should. Here is *Moby Dick* open on my stomach. It's a classic, something I should read and never have. I remember picking it up from a fifty cent bin outside of a bookstore in San Francisco. I bought it at the counter with spare change and then, because it is so compact—one of those drugstore-sized editions—I carried it around in my coat pocket. It felt wonderful to do that: to walk around San Francisco with Herman Melville's *Moby Dick* so close to me.

Here it is again: *Moby Dick* open on my stomach, close to me still.

I picked it up again and sat down on the couch

with grand notions of just diving into it, getting swept up and submerged in the prose, the great American novel. But before I opened to the first page, I decided that I wanted a beer. I stood up and went to the fridge. I opened a beer and took a sip there at the fridge before crossing back across the room. I sat down on the couch again, put my feet up, sipped the beer, and leafed through the yellowed pages of the book to see the size of the type font and how long the first chapter was and how many pages in total there were. My forefinger and thumb rubbing against the pulp of the page as I flipped through, flicking up tiny dust particles and that stagnant damp smell—I sneezed. I closed the book and sneezed again. The wind kicked up outside and the laundry machine turned on. I took a sip of beer.

That is the story of how I am here now.

I am here now. I sneeze and the laundry machine runs. I take a sip of beer.

I think about my day with you tomorrow. It will be the same as it was today and, in that sense, it is already a memory. We will have the same conversation. You will say tell me about yourself and I will shrug, not knowing where to start or what to say. I'll say, I moved here from California and you'll nod, your eyes closed in concentration. California, now that is interesting. And what do your parents do? They're retired, I'll say and you'll smile and look up at me, sounds like the life, you'll say. You'll ask me what I do. What do you mean? I'll say. You'll look down and ask, slowly and deliberately, tapping the table with your hand in order to clarify: what do you do when you're not here with me? You always ask me this and I don't have a good answer. What I do is I spend time with you. This is my job. You ask what do you do? and I don't really have an answer to that other than I come here. I spend time with you, but I can't say that to you. I don't know. I just couldn't.

You ask me What do you do? and I can't bring myself to answer anything.

I shrug. I say something nonsensical, like Oh you know, the usual. Nothing much. I come here in the morning, I leave after lunch. I think about how I go to parties and stand in apartment kitchens, talking to people I kind of know, and they always ask me what do you do? and my response is often rambling and inarticulate as I consider the books I am not reading, the beers I am drinking, the couches I am sitting on.

I just end up talking about you.

I work with an old woman who has dementia, I explain. I go to her house and sit with her and read to her and I take her to lunch and then bring her back home.

That is so interesting, the people say and they ask about you, they want to know who you are and what you're like. They ask me as if I have the answer, like it is possible for me to know the answer and tell them confidently that this is who you are.

Very stubborn—that is always the first thing that comes to mind. I think about how I get your coffee when we are out for lunch, reminding you that you should not put too much sugar into it because sugar is bad for you and you look at me and chuckle, continuing to lift spoon after spoon of white sugar into your cup, saying I didn't know you were such an expert on nutrition.

You are very snarky, too, which goes well with stubborness. I think about how whenever you ask me a question and I respond with a shrug—an I-don't-know—you laugh. You mock my shrug, saying I-da-ho, *Alaska*. You always ask me what my parents are doing that morning and I shrug, I don't know. What do you have planned for this weekend? I shrug, I don't know. You roll your eyes and whistle: I-da-ho, Alaska. You laugh as if it's the first time you told that joke and I nod to say ok ok I get it.

You are outgoing too. I think about how you listen to other people at nearby tables when we're at lunch, how you lean into their conversations—it makes me so uncomfortable but you don't notice.

You sound like very interesting people, you say. Where are you from?

We're from New Jersey, they say and you go, New Jersey! Wonderful! Well, I'm from here and you've picked a wonderful place to visit. You charm them with a smile and then look back at me: Introduce yourself, you say, and I lean in and shake these strangers' hands because you made me and I can feel the heat flattening against the front of my face. I can see them trying to understand the situation: who I am and who you are. You are oblivious to all of this. I grew up here my whole life, you tell them again. They are very polite, saying that it must've been quite special to grow up in such a beautiful place. You nod, yes, oh, it was wonderful, and you ask again, where are you from? And there is a pause—my face is burning and looking down—and the people from New Jersey say, we're up visiting from New Jersey.

New Jersey! Wonderful! And I excuse myself from the table to go pay the check.

I play with my beer can. Clicking the tab. Making that dull, springy sound, that thung-sound. I look at my feet—here I am in my basement room. The buzzer from the laundry machine sounds through the plaster wall. The load is done. I pick up *Moby Dick* from my stomach and lay it on the ground by the couch. I turn the light off above my head and close my eyes.

·ᜭ·   ·ᜭ·   ·ᜭ·

Today is the same.

I read to you. You put your head down and sleep. You snore. Water cracks in your throat. You snore. I keep reading to you though you are not listening. You are loud in your sleep. Water cracks in your throat. Exhale— you whinney with horse lips. You laugh and sleep and I continue to read.

When you wake, you see the book open in my hands and ask What are you reading? Could you read me a story? I'd love to hear a story.

I say ok. I read to you.

Today is the same.

Your head falls. It bobs and eases down to the table slow like a tide going out, water falling back on itself until it is quiet and far away.

Your head is down.

I hear air escaping from your mouth and I stop reading aloud. My throat is tired. Sore. I look at the top of your head. Sit in the silence of the kitchen.

I go on reading to myself, but soon after you lift your head from the table as if the quiet was somehow so loud it woke you.

Did you stop? you ask.

Oh sorry, I thought you were sleeping.

I am not sleeping. I am listening, you say.

Okay, I say.

I go back and start to read again, giving each word a voice as I glance up at you now and then to see if you are sleeping again. I want to stop. My throat feels sore.

Your head is down again. I can not see your face. I feel ridiculous reading aloud to the top of your head but if I stop you will wake. My reading to you is like a spell that keeps you asleep. When I stop, the charm is broken. You wake.

I stop reading and you wake.

Go on, I am listening, you say.

You do not like silence. Even when you sleep you talk. You make small talk in your sleep. Oh wonderful, yes I'm doing wonderfully. The range of your voice fluctuating in pleasant dips and climbs, up and down. I'm doing wonderfully, yes, welcome come in come in, like you are hosting a dinner party. A couple from town knocks at the door, you welcome them in. Come in come in. The house was tidier then. The shelves were ordered and there were no milk crates stuffed with manilla folders and old coats stacked on the floor. The pictures hung straight on the walls. I can't imagine you have many guests now. But I'm sure back then, there were people over every weekend.

I can see you then, in your house, in a nice dress with your hair up, welcoming your guests in. Come in come in and you hug the wife and shake hands with the husband and they come in come in. Their kids have already run around back to the yard to meet your children. They run around the garden and between the apple trees and you can see them, hear their shrill laughs as they chase each other, from the porch where you and your guests drink whiskey and soda and iced tea. There are crackers with cheese. Ice rattles off glasses. Your husband and the other husband stand at the railing looking out over the yard. Your husband points to the grass, then to the driveway recently paved, then to the slice between the trees where you can see the water. The other husband nods. You sit down with the wife and say I'm doing wonderfully, yes, and touch her arm and start to nod as you listen to her, speaking, going on about something, nodding and bobbing your head, smiling, your lipstick on red and your hair pulled back under a band, tidy and blonde and you are listening. You smile and laugh. I can hear your laugh and you say

Go on, I'm listening.

I look up, focus my eyes, and you are smiling at me, nodding me on. Your hair falls in front of your face and with a wrinkled finger you pull the gray lock back behind your ear.

I say sorry and start to read again.

Can you go back, maybe to the beginning of the page?

Ok.

I start to read and you laugh.

Slower—could you go a little slower? I'm so old it is hard to keep up.

I go slower and read louder. I go at an exaggerated pace and I feel like I'm shouting.

You mumble, oh excellent, oh, this is great.

I am reading the story 'Eveline' by James Joyce.

I tell you that Eveline sits at the window and watches as the evening invades her street. I tell you that she leans against the window curtains and inhales the odor of dusty cretonne. I go on, telling you Eveline was tired, watching people move along her street, hearing their footfalls as they moved along her street below her window, oh, how her street has changed over the years—I am telling you all of this when you stop me and ask

What was that word?

What word?

The word you said before. You laugh. You don't know *the word*?

I shake my head.

Here, start at the beginning and go slow.

I go back to the top. I tell you again—and let you know by my tone that I am doing this *again* —that Eveline sits at the window and watches as the evening invades her street and as she leans against the curtains she inhales the odor of dusty cretonne—

Yes. That one. You sound out the word: *Cray*-tone. So interesting. And what does it mean?

I shrug, but you can not see me. You have propped your head up on your chin, but your eyes are closed, pressed together in concentration.

I look back over the first lines. I have no idea what cretonne is.

Maybe it is something in the air, coming up from the street, I say.

You do not respond. You repeat the word.

Cray- tone, you say. Is it French?

I nod. That sounds right. Then I add, Oui oui we might be French.

You laugh and the table shakes. Oh, you're wonderful.

You forget about the word and I continue on with the story. I read it slow. You put your head down and start to breathe heavily. I think that you are probably asleep but I can not stop. You would wake if I stopped. I keep reading. There is an Irish word I can't pronounce, *keogh*, and I pretend it is not there. I don't want you to stop me again. What was that word? Go back a bit…I've never heard such an *interesting* word before. I go on with the story. My voice is loud. I go slow. I am uncomfortable sitting there in my chair. My throat is sore. It is still morning and the sun is strong coming through the glass, hitting my face. I am Eveline at the window feeling tired. I want to lean against the window curtains, inhale the odor of dusty *cray*-tone, and hide my face from the sun.

It is a short story and towards the end, again, the story tells us that Eveline sits at the window. Again, I tell you that Eveline is at the window and this time she is worried about time, about running out of time, and with her head against the curtains she inhales the odor of dusty cretonne and again, you stop me.

What was that word?

I do not respond. My voice hurts from reading out loud.

What was that word? *Cray*-tone?

Yes.

So interesting. *Cray*-tone. Do you know what it means?

No, I don't know.

It sounds French. Is it French?

I pause, then say, Oui oui, we might be French.

You laugh and the table shakes.

Oh, you're wonderful.

I nod and the story ends.

I glance at the clock on the wall and it is almost time to go.

I try to start getting you ready to go into town by 10:30 or so. It takes you a long time to get prepared to leave the house. Sometimes you'll be so tired from your nap, from sitting there in your chair not doing anything, that it will take me fifteen minutes just to get your head up from the table.

I'm up I'm up, you'll say, face down on the table, not getting up. I'm up I'm up, you'll say and then slip back into sleep.

Once I stood over you for 45 minutes calling your name again and again, trying to get you to wake up, to start getting ready to go. I remember glancing at the clock over and over, watching the minutes fall away, thinking how we're late, we should be gone, out the door, as I repeated your name, softer and then more stern: *It's time* to go, trying to get you to lift your head, to wake up.

How did I get so tired? you asked the table, not getting up. You laughed and I was so stressed, trying to get you up as I watched the time go and go and go. I eventually gave up. I called your husband and told him that you were very tired and we couldn't go into town to get lunch. I was so embarrassed. My job consisted of taking an old lady to lunch and I couldn't even do that. I thought your husband would be upset but he wasn't. He just said ok, it's probably because we visited our grandchildren yesterday and you were still tired from that. I said ok, that makes sense. Then I said I was sorry and he said don't be sorry and that he'll be back at the house soon. I hung up the phone and looked at you sleeping there with your head on the table. I remember feeling very warm towards you at that moment. Somehow it took me until then to understand that when I left you after lunch you did not just stop being like I did not just stop being.

You forgot me so I tried my best to forget you.

But now it is really time to go.

Do you want to start getting ready to go? I ask.

Oh, yes, you say. And where will we be going?

We are going to lunch.

Oh, excellent! you say, but do not move.

Great, I say, standing up.

You laugh. Ok, well I'm just going to keep my head down for a couple more minutes and then we'll get ready to go. Ok?

Your voice always goes up when you say ok to me.

Ok, I say.

I am standing over you. I nod and push my chair in.

Ok, well I'll just go get the car ready and then when I come back, you can get up. Sound good?

You laugh for some reason. Sounds good!

I walk into the hallway where your walker is kept and carry it out to the car.

You hate using the walker when we go into town. You are always telling me that you don't need it anymore. I believed you my first week coming here. I told you I had to go get the walker before we went into town and you scrunched up your face and said no no, waving your hand at me, I haven't used that thing in weeks! I shrugged and said ok. I did not know what our days looked like then. I did not know how weak your legs were. You are self-conscious about using it—the walker makes you feel helpless and I understood that. I did not want you to feel helpless. I wanted you to like me. I left the walker in the hallway and I walked you to the car. We drove into town. We parked and I helped you out of the car onto the sidewalk. It was not easy—your legs were wobbly, your weight would not settle neatly onto them. Your balance was bad. I worried that if I pulled too hard on your arm I would hurt you. You chuckled to yourself after you were finally able to stand up, your eyes closed. You took me by the arm and we shuffled our way down the sidewalk towards the cafe where we were having lunch. Your steps were small and I could feel your weight on my arm, how it would suddenly swing out and I'd grab your hand with mine, making sure you wouldn't fall. It was hard for me to walk that slow. You were tired—still tired from the walk through your house to the car, from getting into the car and getting out. You were out of breath. You stopped me, telling me you had to sit down. There was a bench in the park at the end of the block, I said and you looked up the street to try and see it. It's there, I said. It's so close. You can get there. You bit your lip and looked down at your shoes. You kept on, taking more and more breaks and I held you tight by the elbow so you wouldn't lose your balance and fall. You closed your eyes and breathed. The day was warm and you unzipped your fleece. People walked by and glanced at us. You smiled weakly at them, chuckled airly, and I smiled too. People were looking at us. I said your name, told you we were close, we were almost there. We finally got to the bench. You reached out your hand and grabbed the iron arm rest, I eased you down and you fell into the seat. You released a heavy sigh. You chuckled and settled in. I watched your whole body sink into that seat, like a boulder into mud. I dreaded making you get up again. We weren't even at the cafe yet. We still had to cross the park and you would have to walk the whole way.

But we eventually got there. We ordered and you were exhausted while you ate, your arm barely able to hold your sandwich to your mouth. Chewing was a chore. I watched your side sag into your hips, your elbow into your ribs, your chin into your shoulders.

After lunch, I decided I'd leave you for just a moment, run to the car, and bring it around so you wouldn't have to walk again. I told you this plan after we finished eating. You said ok, whatever works for you. I was nervous about leaving you alone. I ran as fast as I could back to the car, drove it back to the cafe, but couldn't find a spot out front, so I double-parked. I threw my hazards on and hurried back into the cafe. You were talking to the waitress. She was sitting down at the table next to you. You were fine. I walked up and asked if you were ready to go?

Go? Already? you said.

We drove back to your house and I walked you inside, back up the hallway to the kitchen table. You sat down and your husband was there, he took me aside and told me that you needed the walker, that you shouldn't go anywhere without it and I nodded. I was hot with shame. I was exhausted. I apologized and I ducked my head back into the kitchen to say bye to you, but you were asleep.

After that I learned to put the walker in the back seat of the car when you were asleep on the table or in the bathroom, getting ready to go. Sometimes you would see it in the back seat and say something about how you hadn't used that thing in ages, but I learned to not respond and you'd forget about it. Sometimes I'd get out of the car after we'd parked and you'd protest saying no no, I don't use that anymore! but I'd unfold it on the sidewalk anyway and, after helping you up onto your feet you would reach out your hand instinctively for balance, finding the handle of the walker. You'd start pushing it down the street and nothing more would be said about it.

I carry the walker out the front door, making sure it doesn't close behind me. It is cold outside but the chill is refreshing. A nice change from the humidity of summer. I load the walker into the back seat of my car and make sure everything is clear from the floor of the front passenger seat.

I linger for a moment in your front yard—the air is so much fresher than inside your home. Everything in there has that stagnant smell. It is an old person's home where nothing changes, objects just sit and are never picked up, rotting to dust. Doors remain closed and rooms are never walked in, never aired out.

I look towards the ocean and the water in the harbor looks heavy today. Waves feathering in the wind. There are no boats out—I imagine many have been brought up onto land in preparation for winter.

A seagull glides through the break in the trees up towards your home. I watch it as it arcs overhead—it comes by often. It will land on your balcony railing and pad around expecting to find some food. Your husband often lays out pieces of bread for it to eat but there are none out now. The bird will linger, it will cry out, and you might wake to it, padding around in its clumsy orange boots. No one else around. The kitchen empty. Just you at the table and the bird at the window.

I hurry back inside. Your head is still down.

I look and the seagull is there as I thought it would be. It's looking in through the glass, expecting bread. I watch it but I will not give into it.

It blinks its black eye, looking at me, but I will not give it what it wants.

Such a handsome bird, you say behind me.

I laugh, if you say so.

I do say so. You smile. You don't?

I just think they're kind of annoying.

Oh. I didn't realize they were annoying. You

chuckle to yourself. You are always chuckling to yourself and I find it very annoying sometimes, like you're laughing at me.

The bird paces up and down the railing, then flies off. I turn back to you and your head is down on the table. I look at the clock. It is time to go. You should get up. I have this urge to suddenly clap and stomp my feet, shout Hey! so your head jolts up and you wake without me having to draw you gently from your sleep. I want to just slam a book on the table and announce We're leaving! to you, but of course I don't do any of that. I stand over you, not knowing what to do. I wait with my hands ridiculously on my hips, like a parent: I'm not mad, I'm *disappointed*. But it is ridiculous, we have nowhere to be. Why rush you out the door to rush you to lunch to rush you out of lunch, we have to go hurry now, we have to get you back.

I relax my shoulders. I look at the clock and sit back down.

I will give you five more minutes.

Put on your coat, I say.

You do not want to wear the coat, I can see that, but you need to wear it. Here it is. I am holding it open for you.

Put it on, it is cold out. I was just outside.

You look past the coat in my hands to the chair at the end of the table piled with your collection of sweaters and fleeces. You shuffle over to the pile and with one hand you pick up each fleece by its scruff, examining it, looking it up and down like you're shopping at a department store. You size up the orange fleece, then the green.

Oh these are wild, you say.

Those are too thin, I say. You're going to need a heavier coat. I gesture towards the window. It is too cold for those. The sky is overcast. A breeze howls and pulls some leaves from the trees to prove my point, but you ignore me. You look at the powder blue fleece and settle on it.

Let's try this one, you say and I tell you again that it is too cold. You'll need to wear the heavier coat. Here I am holding it out for you, I can help you put it on.

Oh, but that one is so black and so heavy, you say, shuffling back to your chair, the blue fleece hanging from your hand clenched at your hip. You lean heavily on the table for balance.

You can carry that coat you got and if I need it I'll let you know, ok?

Your voice goes up and I can tell you are getting annoyed with me. You are telling me I am not a child, I can figure out what I wear on my own.

I say ok, knowing exactly what will happen. I will open the front door and you'll feel the frost in the air and the bite of the wind and say Jesus, it's freezing out! You'll ask for the heavier coat and in the cramped entryway, I'll have to work the coat onto your back, pulling your arms through, getting the damn thing over your shoulders.

You sit down and hand me the blue fleece. I tell you it'd be easier for me to help you if you were standing up.

You say, no it's okay we can get it on while I sit.

Ok.

I unzip the zipper and hold it open for you. You lean forward and stretch your right arm behind you over the back of the chair. Your cheek presses against the table as you make your fingers into a point like the head of a spade and you dig for the sleeve. You miss it. You miss it again, bending your arm back blindly, thinking you have the armhole now before pushing your hand down into the chair. You huff and shift. The table moves. I take your wrist and lightly pull it back to help. I can feel the tension in your arm, it hums from your wrist to your shoulder. It feels like the wing of a small bird. I have your wrist and I think this is like putting a fleece on a chicken.

It'd be easier if you stood up—but as I say it, you find the sleeve and push your hand through.

There, you say with relief and triumph. You shift your weight and start on the other arm. It is the same. You do not find the sleeve any easier and I help again.

Finally, it is on.

Alright, let's head out, I say and you sit up and work on the zipper. I watch you as you try to lock the ends together. They are too small, and your fingers are too swollen. You close your eyes and laugh.

Can you help me with this? and I say sure.

You stand up and I crouch, holding my breath. Your perfume smells like baby powder and stale white wine. You wear too much of it and it is old by the looks of the dust accumulated on the bottle and it has probably gone bad, if that is a thing that happens to perfume. Before we head out, you always grab the bottle, close your eyes and liberally spritz your neck. The smell wraps around my face like a scarf. I smother a cough. Please don't, I say to myself as you spray it, angling your chin up, turning your neck, spraying it again.

I quickly bring the zipper ends together and pull the zipper a quarter of the way. Alright, I got it started for you, I say, standing up straight and stepping away.

You're wonderful.

You zip the zipper up to your throat and we head down the hallway. I walk in front of you with the coat and your purse. I stop at the three steps that lead down to the front door entryway and look back. You have your hand out to the wall for balance, watching your feet as you walk.

Do you have my purse?

Yes.

Are my glasses in my purse?

Yes.

You stop and look at me. Your left hand is against the wall and your other arm crooks in at the elbow. Its hand rests on your thigh. You do not use this hand for anything. I don't know why, but it is no good.

Did you check?

Yes but I can check again.

I unzip the bag and make a show of looking through it. I see the glasses in their soft case.

Yes, they're in here.

You're wonderful, you say, sighing deeply.

I help you down the steps. The entryway is crowded with both of us in it. The large plastic plant with paper leaves pushes me into you. I inhale the perfume. I have the purse and coat slung over my arm as I hold your elbow and open the front door. I use my back to keep the door open and the air comes in.

Jesus, it's freezing out, you say, stopping on the threshold. You look at the coat in my arms. I want to put that on.

I can't help but say I told you so and you act like you didn't hear me. You turn around so I can pull your arms through and get the coat onto your shoulders.

Does it have a hood? you ask.

I nod, knowing that you can not see me. I turn you around, button the coat and throw the hood over your head.

The coat is huge and it hangs straight off your shoulders. You look like a football player with it on, draped over heavy pads swallowing your neck.

I open the door and take your hand to help you out. The wind picks up and you grip my hand tight and roll my knuckles. It feels much colder than when I was out before. I close the door and we cross the yard to my car sitting in the driveway.

Is that yours? you ask.

There she is, I say.

You move quickly because of the cold and you know that you are not going far. I open the door and help you into the car. You say oh, you're such a gentleman and I say just doing my job. I steady the door and try to block the wind coming up the hill as you lift your foot up and into the front seat. You manage it, but get caught with your head ducked low so you won't bang your head on the top of the door frame. You laugh and huff, shifting the foot you have planted on the driveway, trying to figure out a way to get that leg to follow the other. I offer to take your other hand but you ignore it. You have one foot in and one foot out and your upper body is folded at your stomach to protect your head. You chirp in discomfort, your shoe scuffles against the loose gravel of the driveway. I don't know how else to help you. I hold onto the door and finally, you just fall into place.

Very smooth, I say.

You laugh, but you are exhausted. I place your purse between your feet and I grab the seat belt and reach over you to buckle you in. I hold my breath. I hear the click of the buckle and stand up.

Ok, I say. I close the door fast and get in behind the wheel. The car has lost all of its heat from the morning drive, but it is nice to be out of the wind. You are breathing heavily, I smile because your coat is bunched up around your head and I can barely see you except for your nose and forehead and knotted tangle of hair. I turn on the car and the heater hums.

Ok, let's get going, I say and start to back out of the driveway. Johnny Cash's *American V: A Hundred Highways*, my only CD, plays from the speakers and you coo in pleasure.

You recognize the voice. Oh, is this Johnny Cash? you ask.

Yes, I say.

I love Johnny Cash, and you start to sing in a high, wavering voice.

You know all the words. They stay with you from day to day, and you sing along as we drive into town.

II.

To the Lighthouse

THE LEAVES FROM the trees are down. Their branches are so bare it looks as if they are shrinking back into their trunks and the trunks themselves are receding into the ground.

The trees are returning to their sapling days, back to their seeds, then nothing.

Beyond their bones is the harbor and the town. We can see it all now that the leaves are down and the trees are shrinking.

You are sleeping and I am killing time before we must head into town by looking out the window and finding things with my eyes. There is the harbor. There is the town. It is a clear day. The crispness of fall had cleared away the haze and warping wet of summer in the air and now we look out the window and can see clearly through winter's cold.

There is the lighthouse. I see it, out there past the town's neck, at the end of a rocky island point, pushing its finger out into the ocean, and I think oh, I'll read *To The Lighthouse* because of course, it'd be perfect to read because we can see the lighthouse from the kitchen window now that it is winter and the leaves are down.

I go to the bookshelf in the hall and take the copy you have down—I know where it is, I have flipped through its pages before—and walk back to the kitchen.

I have never read Virginia Woolf and I am excited because she is one of the best—everyone says—and it's really embarrassing that I've gone this long without reading her. I decide I am going to love this book and sit down heavily with it in my hands. The small chair crackles and pops adjusting to my weight and you shift across the table from me. You mumble wet-lipped and laugh—you are always mumbling and laughing while you sleep.

You say something about a sweater.

Oh yes...the sweater...it's lovely.

You start to snore. Loud, too. You put your back into it when you snore. I can't help but laugh as the air clogs up your nose and you sputter like a lawn mower.

I open the book, pass over the foreword by Eudora Welty, and find the start of section one. It is called "The Window" and I think this is perfect, for I am reading next to a window and out beyond it is a lighthouse.

The book begins and Mrs. Ramsey speaks, saying something like yes, tomorrow we will go to the lighthouse. "But you'll have to be up with the lark," she says and her boy, James, is filled with excitement and anticipation for an adventure is promised. To the lighthouse! They'll have to sail and it will take all day.

The book begins and the beginning goes on for some time—it is a long sentence. I find myself reading it fast, gaining speed, because it is not stopping. The words roll on and roll on and my body tenses, my spine straightens as the words continue on. I am sinking in, no—floating away. I am not even reading. None of these words mean anything. I feel a rope tighten across my shoulder blades. A flat pain across my forehead. My teeth are clenched and I don't know why—relax. I sit back, release my jaw, and exhale. I lift the book up from the table and hold it by its covers. If I pull hard and out I could split it like a wishbone. I want to do just that and I don't know why. I find this anger in me. It comes from somewhere inside of my body and I do not know it or recognize it until it is nearly through my skin and jumping out of me. It makes me want to do things quick and violent: break a glass, pull a book apart. The snapping of its spine will snap mine, get it out of its rigidity, release its clench—relax.

I shudder as a shiver passes through me like a breeze through branches, dry wood rattling.

Relax.

I look up and see you. You cough, out there in your sleep, across the table from me.

I am in your life, deep in your home, and you are old and sick and dying and it is overwhelming. It is too much. Being here tightens me up. I don't know how to get through this, how to live a life, and do it good and beautiful. I look out the window and there is the ocean, deep and endless, and thinking about the years, the months, the coming day even, feels like being dropped in the middle of that ocean out there. I look at you and there is a whole life between us.

I get annoyed and angry at the smallest things.

You ask me questions—you've already asked me that before.

You sleep all the time—get up! You're tired all the time because you sleep all the time.

You say read to me—can't I just get a moment of peace? I want to be alone.

I am young and you are old. You dream about what you have already had in life and I can only imagine what might come, or what might not come, and it is all waiting.

My mind slips its mooring and floats away. I am sinking down and floating away. My eyes unfocus on the page in front of me.

It is impossible that life ends. It is impossible that it winds down and stops. It is impossible that it is here and then it is gone.

Out the window, imagine the water pulling back, draining away, gone.

Maybe I am mad at you for that.

Maybe I am a little jealous of you for that.

When I look at you and I am looking out at you, as if through a window, and there is no end to your breadth and depth. There is no end to your ever-changing skin.

"It's due west," said the atheist Tansley and I do not know how I got here. I scan back the couple of pages I apparently just read. Tansley is talking about the lighthouse—the one James wants to go to and his mother, Mrs. Ramsey, says yes, of course he can go, and on it goes. There is so much joy until James's father, Mr. Ramsey, says "But..." He says something like but a trip to the lighthouse won't be fine, and suddenly that joy in the boy becomes rage, murderous rage. Then Mrs. Ramsey, over her knitting, says "But...it may be fine" and her thoughts go on about her knitting until Tansley the atheist says "It's due west" and he's talking about the lighthouse.

We went to the lighthouse last summer.

I remember how it was hot and you complained. I remember watching you push your walker up the sidewalk from the cafe to the car, stopping after every couple shuffled steps or so to sigh dramatically, hanging your tongue and rolling your eyes.

Did you purposely park this far? you asked.

But of course, I said, looking back at you. I wanted to make sure you'd be miserable.

You laugh and then the laugh is gone.

It is so hot out—

I know, we're almost there.

I just wilt in the heat.

I know.

You stopped to squint up the street at the line of cars parked there.

Which one is yours?

It's the red one.

You counted with your hand, one eye almost closed.

That one five away?

I looked and counted.

Yes.

Jesus, did you purposely park this far away?

It's not that far, I said.

I kept walking, swinging your purse as I moseyed on, looking back at you and straining my neck as if that would help pull you along, roll you along, and get you going faster. Cars drove by and their passengers stared at us. We must've been a strange sight—a young man and an old woman bickering back and forth with one another as they shuffle up the sidewalk.

We finally got to the car. I steadied the door as you fell into the front seat. Very smooth, I said. I checked the time and there was still some time to kill before your husband said to meet him back at the house. I suggested we go for a drive. As long as I don't have to get out of the car, you said. Okay, I said, smiling, and reached across you to roll down your window to get you some air. You sank into the chair, the chest strap of the seatbelt holding you up as your head drooped like a sunflower over your shoulder. Your eyes were closed. Your shoulders rose and fell as you tried to find your breath.

I followed the main road up the hill and out of town and decided to head towards the lighthouse. You could not see it from your kitchen window then because the trees were filled out with leaves, but I knew it was there. I had seen pictures of it and had got glimpses of it on drives. At that point in the summer, I had not been working for you long—the town felt new and I still wanted to explore. I knew the direction the lighthouse was in and I figured it would not be hard to find if I just stuck to the coast.

As I drove, the wind blew your hair up, making it wild, but you did not seem to mind. I remember you laughing as you pulled a strand from your mouth. You were tired but you were happy, leaning with the curve in the road, just sitting.

A couple of turkeys crossed the road ahead of us and I slowed down to watch as the birds passed and disappeared into the brush.

Those are some ugly birds, I said.

You smiled and said, Yes, but they're delicious.

I turned down a residential road that ended at a dirt lot, looking over a coved beach. This was a local spot. It was secluded. The beach in town was crowded with tourists while the sand in front of us was peppered with very few. A handful of men and women sat back in chairs. Children dug in the sand and teased the water. A dog splashed in the foam and barked. From the end of the beach, a trail of rocks peppered out into the water, ending in a flat, circular slate topped with the lighthouse.

Eastern Point, you said, sitting up to see over the dashboard.

There it is, I said, thinking it was not all that exciting, but it was a pleasant day and it was nice to be outside. Out from us was nothing but blue water and blue sky. I remember it being so clear that day the sky felt heavy, resting on us like a full glass.

I think I learned to swim at this beach, you said.

Not a bad place to learn.

No, not at all. You chuckled, sitting back in the seat. My father would walk me and my sister out, one in each arm, until the water was up to our feet and then he'd drop down and the water would jump to our stomachs and we'd scream! It was such a shock. We loved that. And then he'd drop us again and we'd scream again. Oh, he was wonderful. We'd say, again daddy again and he would. He'd dip us deeper and deeper with the water climbing up our chests, my sister and I screaming the whole way, giggling with excitement. Then, when the water was deep enough, he'd say Okay, get ready girls 'cause we're going down, and we'd take one big breath before we all dropped into the water together.

Your face was sharp looking out at the lighthouse. Color had spread across your face as you told that story. The skin around your eyes tightened and the crow's feet and pockmarks along your cheek seemed to clear away. You sighed and looked up at me and your face had changed. It was fuller, maybe, full of color. I remember seeing something pass through your eyes: the skin of something dark, the wetback of some breaching animal. It broke through the water, turned the skin of it foamy white, then disappeared. It sounds strange but I'm sure I saw something there. It was in your eyes. It made you sharp and young again and I felt like an imposter. Someone who was out-of-place. Someone half there. And then, just as quickly, your face changed back to what I knew before. You became the old lady again. You closed your eyes and chuckled, sinking back into your seat, and I relaxed.

For a moment, I was dropped into something that had no end.

I looked at the clock. It was time to go.

Alright let's move on, I said, shifting the car in reverse.

Yes, you said. I'm starving.

You're starving? We just ate!

We did?

You got a roast beef sandwich. Half of it is still in your bag.

You're kidding?

I shook my head, looking back over my shoulder.

You laughed: I guess I forgot that I wasn't hungry

anymore.

I guess so, I said, pulling onto the road back into town.

You are snoring and there's no point trying to read with you going on like that. I close the book and hide it under a stack of papers on the table so you will not see it when you wake. I do not want you to ask me about it.

I check the time and it is not quite time. It feels like it's been winter forever though the first snow has yet to fall. The sky has stayed a bitter gray and the ocean there is the same color. Everything is granite, a cold stone. And there is the lighthouse—out past the trees, across the harbor, and far away.

I come in and sit down at the table and you are mumbling in your sleep. You wake up and say, my goodness I'm tired, isn't it awful how tired I am? before your head drops down to the table again.

Our days seem to blend together.

How do you sleep like that? your body bent over itself, head on the hard table.

You ask me where are you from? Where do you live now? What do you do? and I can never seem to answer in a way that you'll remember.

What do you do? What do you want to do? *I-da-ho*, Alaska.

You show me a picture of your father—it's always there, propped up and framed in front of you on the table. Have I shown you this before? you ask. Such a handsome man. I can see the resemblance, I say, handing back the picture and you take it and tell me that he was in the military and no-nonsense and when you'd say, I think so daddy, as a little girl, he'd furrow his brow and say, you're not supposed to *think*, you're supposed to *know*. That makes you laugh remembering that now. How is it that it is this phrase that sticks? After all this time, you pick up the picture of your father smiling in a field with an open shirt collar and a pipe proud in his mouth and he is young, too young for you to have known him like this, and there are all these memories and photographs of your father housed in your body and mind and within these rooms, but you emerge with that line, the line: *you're not supposed to think, you're supposed to know.* You're not supposed to think, you're supposed to know floods your memory when you see the picture there in front of you. You look at it and sink into it, letting the tide charge up the beach and cover you. Your father leans down over you as you look up at him, a child, full of uncertainty, or just fear, and you answer I think so daddy in a high, fragile voice, and he will have none of it, he furrows his brow and says you're not supposed to think and you know how the line goes—he's said it to you enough so that you know exactly what he'll say and how he'll respond and it's at the point where even when you do know what he'll say you can't help but say I think so daddy to him because that is your line. It is a reflex, it's comfortable. You say your line, even though it is not true—you do not think, you do know—but to hear his line in his voice is comfortable. You're not supposed to think you're supposed to know, he says and you repeat that to me now whenever you look at the photograph in front of you.

You laugh. When I was a girl I'd say, I think so daddy, and my father would always say, You're not supposed to think, you're supposed to know.

I smile, but I think it's a stupid saying. It is good to think, to admit that you don't know. It is okay to be unsure. It is okay, I tell myself.

But I admit, I often find myself saying I *think* when I actually know.

You ask where your husband is and I say, I think he went to run some errands in town. You ask when he'll be home and I say, I think around one o'clock. You chuckle and shake your head. Have I ever told you what my father would say to me when I was a girl?

Somehow that phrase has stayed with you, but now the roles have changed. You say his line while I say yours.

You are delicate, setting the photograph of your father down on the table in front of you, straightening it if it is even slightly crooked. It must be facing you so that you can see it. You look at it for a moment before you lay your head down again.

It is when you put your head down that I become comfortable here.

I come in the morning, walk up the hall and sit down in my chair across from you. We say our hellos, we say our lines, and you eventually drop your head and sleep.

I sit still across from you.

I look out the window and watch the birds. I open a book to read, looking up occasionally when you make a sound, ignoring you if you say something nonsensical like I like your sweater when I am not wearing a sweater—you are just dreaming.

I am comfortable doing the same thing and saying the same thing each day, letting each day pass over us and through us, the weather being the only thing changing between us. You wake up and show me the photograph of your father and I say I can see the resemblance and you nod and you laugh. You tell me again the story of him saying you're not supposed to think, you're supposed to know and I nod along, not adding my own thoughts but just nodding along until you put your head down again so I can go back to sitting and reading and looking out the window. I am just nodding along. I sink back in my chair, cross one leg over another with a book open in my lap and look up at you occasionally, briefly, stealing a glance. I look at you and you are not looking at me. You have sunk into the table and have become another feature of that unchanging landscape. I look out at you and your skirt of hair fans out over the plastic dinner tray as it always does. There is your water glass. There are the unlit candles, the stacks of dishware, the stack of books. There are the two ceramic doves with their wings cocked behind their backs and there is the hump of your shoulder and there is the phone and the magazines and mail. I sit back and there you are. I know you like I know the objects on the table. Everything is in its place.

I look out the window and there is the harbor and there is the town and there is the lighthouse.

I am comfortable. I have my copy of *Moby Dick* open on my lap but I don't read it. I look out the window and the sky is graying over the ocean, like a cloth soaking up water.

Loud knock on my door. I wake to it—the loud knock and a voice.

Get up, kid. Come on.

The voice is low and harsh and I am up at it, pulling on the pants I had draped over the back of my desk chair. I know who it is—there is only one person who comes to my basement room. I open the door and Gus stands there in his Carhartt jacket, stamping his boots like a horse against the ground, hiding a cigarette in his hand. He's the groundskeeper for the property I live on. I live rent-free if I help him with yard work and other random jobs around the place. They are just chores. Mindless tasks like changing light bulbs and raking leaves. I don't make money but I earn my keep. I like that balance. It is even and simple.

And there is Gus at the door, kicking the caked snow off his boots in the early morning.

Get dressed kid, he says, throwing a red thumb over his shoulder as if to say hop to it let's get going don't you know snow is coming down. He doesn't wait for me. He stomps back out the door into the cold. I glance out my window and it's true, snow is coming down and by the looks of the half-buried window it has been coming down for some time now. I rush to get dressed. I grab my coat and hat and gloves and go out in it.

The woods are white and covered. Nothing is out there beyond the house but snow. None of the brush and thicket, the fallen logs and sitting rocks—all of it is snow and even the trees and their branches are clothed in the soft, sticking white. I stand there and watch the snow fall and it is like the flat gray of the sky is crumbling into pieces and reforming on the ground. I stand there and there is no sound. Winter is quiet. I trudge around to the front of the house where Gus sits in the front seat of the steaming truck, idling at the end of the driveway with a yellow plough fixed to its front fender.

Grab a shovel, he says and there's his big red thumb going over his shoulder again to the truck bed. He breathes out smoke and it is so cold that it is like he is exhaling a cloud from his lungs. Dig out the front door and the driveway while I plough the long driveway and once that's done we'll salt it down so it won't build up again.

Sounds good, I say and grab a shovel.

He drives up the road and lowers the plough at the mouth of the long driveway that winds up the hill to the main house and barn. The truck is in low gear. It is loud and harsh as he inches forward and the plough grinds against the gravel of the driveway. The sound is like his voice, his throat grinding up against each word as it comes out of his mouth. I'm part Polish, part Irish and part alleycat! he always says. Kid, I'm a fucking stray! He always says, and I nod and laugh when he says that, not knowing really what to do or say in response. I just smile and nod and try to stay out of his way. Sometimes when we're working together he'll ask Why are you so fuckin quiet, kid? And then he'll carry on talking, not waiting for my answer.

I drop the shovel down into the snow at the end of the driveway and lift. The snow is light and breaks away in big pieces. I toss the load to the side and continue on. I work quickly and the progress is quick and evident. It feels good to work hard before I've had coffee or breakfast. It's a refreshing way to wake up—it involves the whole body and feels instinctual. I don't even know the time, but it must be early. I just drop the shovel into the snow and toss it to the side. Legs spread and feet planted, I dig forwards, further in, until I have cleared out the front path to the front door. I salt the walkway and then go to the tenants' cars parked to the side and brush off the snow from the hoods and windshields and tops of their cars. I stand their wipers up if they had forgotten to do so the night before. I look back towards the house with its four stories, hoping that no one will think I'm messing with their car. It is a strange building, a white rectangle built into a hill so the top floor is level with the top of the hill and the basement floor is level with the bottom of it. I have to lean back against a car to see its roof. The sky powders my face—I squint into it. I imagine someone in each of the wide-eyed windows, transfixed by the view. It'd be nice to be up there. Warm. Nothing else to do but put your chin in your hand and watch the outside swirl and move beyond the glass. Nothing else to do but be still and warm and watch as snow falls, burying this world.

I look over to the neighbor's property and he is shoveling his driveway. I wave but he doesn't wave back. His head is down on the work at hand.

What do you do on these snowy days?

The same things you do on any other day, I suppose. You sit in your chair at the kitchen table. You eat. You sleep. But it is different because I am not there. Your husband has not gone to run errands, he stays at home and is there with you and I am not there. But you do not know that I am not there and you do not know that this snow day is any different than any other day. For you, this different day is a normal day, a day that has been normal for years. You look around and you are in your kitchen in the house you grew up in and your husband is there next to you reading the paper, or you can hear him below tinkering in the garage, or padding around the other room. Everything is as it always is and was. Nothing is different. Here is your life. You look up from a nap and your husband is rubbing your back absentmindedly as he watches the news. What's the word? you ask and he says same ol' same ol'. No news. Outside, snow falls. The stone wall is covered. You watch as someone shovels out your driveway. You think it's your son and say something about how you think he should come inside for some tea to warm up and your husband says no that's the neighbor's boy, he shovels out all the driveways on the block. Well invite him in to warm up anyway, you say, lowering your head to the table, it must be freezing out.

I look down and snow is already starting to cover the driveway I just shoveled. The ground I uncovered is already white and gone and I tell myself that it is okay, you knew that would happen, it is okay. I tell myself that it's good that I cleared some of the snow away now so it wouldn't get out of hand and make the work ten times worse later. I walk up the driveway, leaving footprints, and the snow continues to fall and it is beautiful but I wish it'd stop. I did all this work and I want there to be proof, at least for a little while longer. I want to see proof of the work I put in. Here is the driveway I shoveled, but no—it is gone now.

I walk up the road with my shovel and turn up the long driveway towards the barn. The gravel is ploughed, the snow is flattened and packed hard so I can walk it easily. There are tire tracks and the lateral marks of the plough—I follow them up to the opened barn where the truck sits parked outside of it, still steaming and running idle, as Gus shovels a mixture of salt and dirt into an old laundry detergent bucket.

The fuck took ya so long kid? but he winks, his cigarette bobs. I trade the snow shovel for a spade and start to fill another bucket. We load them onto the bed, the tail-gate is down and the buckets are heavy. I'm starting to feel the cold in my feet. Gus wants to salt the long driveway fast, he wants to get the salt down so it melts away some of the snow now so it's not so bad later. I'm not sure how well that will work but I say ok.

This driveway is a bitch, he says into his cigarette.

He tells me to sit on the tailgate and spread the salt as he drives. He'll go slow, he says, give the salt a good heave, and he shows me how by tilting the bucket with one hand and with the other he swipes out from the bucket in a wide swing that sends a spray of salt and dirt over the ground. Really heave it out there, he says, and I nod and say I got it. I sit up on the tailgate with my feet dangling off and situate the bucket so it is propped next to me. Gus shouts out the window that he's going and the truck rocks into movement. I feel myself slide a little and grab on.

Spread it kid! Come on! he shouts from the cab and the road starts to move below my feet. I get to work, swinging my arm out, sending the salt and dirt across the road in boughed arcs that pepper across the packed snow. Faster kid! And I try to pick up my pace but it is hard holding the bucket because it is heavy with packed wet sand and salt and my arm is already tired from the rapid succession of throwing my arm out over and over again. I can feel the ache in my elbow and my gloves are already soaked through. My fingers are cold and I keep going, but it is slow and hard to spread the salt out along the driveway in any substantial way. The snow keeps coming down. Go slower, I shout, but Gus does not hear and soon we are at the bottom of the driveway. Come on kid, he shouts back and gets out of the car to show me again how he wants it done. Fast, he says. Really fast, and he is frustrated, I can tell, damn kid, and the smoke from his cigarette blows up into his eye, making it squint, and I nod, I got it, but go a little slower, I say and he says nothing to that, getting back into the cab. The truck jumps forward again, this time up the driveway. I am faster now and my arm is more numb to the movement and the pain it causes. I sow the salt and dirt, spreading it out over the snow. The cold granules scrape my fingertips through my glove. I dig deeper into the bucket as I throw out more and more and eventually there is none left. Done, I shout, holding up the bucket. Gus stops and I put the empty bucket behind me and slide up the full one, taking a moment to secure myself on the tailgate and position the bucket so that I can get to the dirt easily and quickly. Gus starts to drive. I'm not ready, I shout and he shouts Jesus Christ kid! And the snow is still falling and it seems to be falling thicker now and I can't imagine that what we're doing now will make much of a difference. I look back and can barely see the dark brown freckles of dirt I just sent out across the snow. Okay, I shout and we start to move again. We get to the top of the driveway and halfway back down again before the second bucket runs out. Done, I shout and Gus stops the car. I drop down from the tailgate and go up to the cab. His elbow hangs from the window and he swears to himself.

Snow's not letting up. This doesn't fucking matter.

I nod and he lets out one more fuck.

Get in the back and I'll drive ya down.

I hop back onto the tailgate and he drives on down the hill to the main road. He's going fast and I can tell he's frustrated. I'm cold and tired and happy to be done. The woods on either side of the road are covered—I had never seen it like this before. The snow blankets and shrouds, it rounds the features off, dulling the landscape, making it so inviting I forget my frustration. Here is this blank and clean beauty: the swell and drift of the bright snow between dark trees.

I get off the truck at the end of my driveway. Gus pulls away without a wave. The snow has erased any evidence of the shoveling I did before. Soon I'll have to shovel it again. I stand there for a moment and the snow lands on my open glove. Flakes collect on my sleeve and do not melt. If I walked out into the woods and stood in one spot and did not move I would eventually be covered and gone and I would not be seen until spring. I take off my gloves and go around the house to the basement door. I kick off the snow caked to my boots and step inside. The laundry machine is running in the other room, tapping against the wall of my small dug-out home.

In the morning, I wake and it has snowed even more during the night. The window is nearly covered and the drift pressed against the glass lights up my room. I get dressed in its blue light.

I walk out to my car and it is hidden by snow and the driveway is unshoveled. It is going to take longer than I expected to get on the road. I look at my watch. I'm not going to make it to your house in time. A wind picks up and it is bitterly cold. I swear into my coat collar. The snow around me winks with ice. I clear off the windshield, the mirrors, the windows, and the hood, then I start to dig from the rear bumper of my car towards the road. The driveway is long and the snow is heavier today. The top of it is frozen, giving it a crust. I dip my knees and shove the shovel into the packed snow and lift a load into the planter between our driveway and the neighbor's. I lift and heave and feel the strain on my back. I am sore from yesterday. I have to pick away at the snow and break it into chunks to heave off to the side. I dig two tracks for my wheels to follow down to the road. I go back to the car and start it—the engine turns slowly because of the cold. I put it in reverse, hold the clutch down and gently press the gas but the tires spin out. I try again but the car does not budge. I can smell rubber. I keep the car running and dig the wheels out more. I bend down and I see the patches of ice and I think well maybe more snow would help it gain traction. I pack snow under the wheels and try again. The car moves slightly before rolling back into its original divot. I swear again. I put the car in neutral and try to rock it free but of course that does not work. My feet slip. I can't get firm enough footing. I have to clear more snow away. I grab the shovel and work fast. Shovel after shovel into the planter, I don't bother to lift with my knees, I slip again, dumping snow into the planter between our driveway and the neighbor's. I hear someone's voice as I work. I keep going but again the voice. Someone says, hey you better! and I stop my digging to look up and it's the neighbor—I've seen her around but never spoken to her. She's sticking her head out of her second floor window, talking to me. Better not, she says, and I look up at her and it takes a beat for me to understand that what she is saying is better not be putting snow into her driveway. You do that and I'll tell my husband, she threatens. I look at her and nod. She nods and I say ok. She closes her window and I start to shovel again, shaking my head, swearing into my coat collar Jesus Christ, goddamn lady—I wish I had said that to her— Jesus Christ goddamn lady and it is so cold and I'm going to be late to get to your house. I clear the path and try to reverse the car again. The tires churn and I push down on the gas, saying come on dammit and the tires churn and spit black snow and I smell rubber and I throw my weight against the back of my chair to try and get the car to move and it doesn't and I'm so completely angry and frustrated, I swear loud and into the steering wheel as I let go of the gas feeling this anger rise up in me and I want to hit some-thing I really do I grind my teeth and clench my fist and I want to hit something to help release this heat in me and

I'm so mad and I sit up against the steering wheel press myself against it and punch the windshield.

I open my mouth, unclench my jaw. My face is hot.

I punched the windshield and now there is a crack with a chambered center where my knuckle hit. It stretches across the glass. I look at it and swear. I go cold. I am so embarrassed. I do not believe it, how could I have let that happen? I look away, then look back. The crack is still there, it looks like it's growing across my eye-line. I take a deep breath and of course then, when it is too late, I remember the bucket of salt kept by the basement door that's been there this whole time, that is always there. I go get it, swearing at myself, and I spread salt beneath the wheels and try again and the tread of the tires grip the grain—I can hear the grind and crunch—and the car starts to move. It rolls down the driveway and out onto the road. I swear at myself as I wind through the neighbor-hood. I speed on the highway towards your house. The sky is cloudless and blue. I try to see past the crack across my windshield. I try to erase it and focus on the road and how the trees along the road are white and black like shaded bones, but I can't help it. The crack stretches out across my eye-line. It is getting longer, I think, and there is nothing I can do to fix it now. It is there now, lengthening across my windshield, and I am so embarrassed and frustrated. What the hell. Goddamn. I charge up the highway, trying to get further and further away from the morning.

I knock on the door. I sing my hello. I walk up the long hallway and you are there.

Oh hello, I did not know someone was coming.

Here I am, I say.

Yes, you say. There you are. I'm just going to put my head down, and you do. You use your chin to move the dinner tray closer to you. You lay your cheek onto the tray like it's a pillow. Some strands of hair fall quiet and slow. They are in no rush to catch up with the rest of your head, lagging behind like a fishing line following a lure into water. I watch these hairs fall. They cast out from the blue line of skin at the top of your hand and find themselves, without a splash, in your water glass.

Today's water is yesterday's.

Lint floats on its surface.

You have your head down and your eyes are closed, but I can tell you are restless today. You are not still and you have not settled into sleep. You chirp and flinch and chuckle in your way that means you are uncomfortable. I take my copy of *Moby Dick* out of my backpack, hoping that you will eventually sink into something deep and still.

I open the book and there is the first line: Call me Ishmael, and you shift again and the table shakes. Under your breath you say I'd love some coffee. Oh, I'd love a nice, hot cup of coffee. You suck in and let loose a short sigh that seems to lift your head. Your eyes point at me. Your pupils are small like the tip of a pen.

You say I could really go for a cup of coffee.

Yes. Coffee sounds good right now.

Doesn't it? I could murder a cup.

I smile but say nothing. I look back down at the book in front of me. I am not reading it, I just don't want to make you coffee. That is what you are getting at—I know because you've done this before—you want me to make you some but I don't want to. I'd have to get up, dig around for a kettle. I'd have to turn on the stove. I'd have to find the jar of instant coffee mix and wash off a spoon. Besides, I don't know where anything is in this kitchen. It's disorganized. Your husband is not one to tidy and neither are you. You would want sugar. I do not want to give you sugar. You take sugar in your coffee, or take coffee with your sugar. I am supposed to try and curb your sugar intake. That's what your husband told me to do. I told you that once and you looked at me in disgust: I don't give a damn what my husband says!

I have made coffee for you before and you made a big show of putting spoon after spoon of sugar into the cup. I said, you probably shouldn't put that much sugar in your coffee and you giggled, you were so happy I had said that. You winked, tongue out, watching the spoon go to the cup, and said oh, I think I'll be just fine.

Sugar is not good for you, I said.

Oh really? I had no idea! You laughed at that. My father always said sugar would give you pinworms.

What is a pinworm? I asked.

I don't know! and you ladled more sugar into your cup.

You say again I'd love some coffee. You gesture vaguely over your shoulder without lifting your head from the table, there should be some somewhere.

I don't think your husband wants us to use the stove, and I hear how lame this excuse sounds as I say it.

You snort: I don't give a damn what my husband says! I can do whatever I want in this kitchen. Where the hell does he get off telling me what to do in my kitchen?

You enjoy being outraged. You like getting in a good huff. I know this and it annoys me because it feels like it is coming at my expense—you are making fun of me. I take a breath and pause. I want to say great then, make your own damn cup of coffee! I don't know where anything is anyway. Just get up and do it yourself, it's not that hard. Just do something about it!

Instead I say that we can get coffee when we head into town. We can get a cup at the cafe.

I don't want a cup of coffee then, I want a cup of coffee now. Why is it so hard to get a cup of coffee in my own kitchen?

I try to ignore you, but you are right, of course. It shouldn't be this hard, but I look down at my book. Call me Ishmael, I read. The moment will pass. I feel you looking at me but the moment will pass. These types of things tend to go away with you if I just let it sit. Let it sit and don't stir the pot. You will probably forget what we were arguing about. We were not really arguing—just leaving a lot of things unsaid. You do not *need* coffee. I am not keeping anything important from you. I glance up from my book and you are looking at me and I can tell that this is not just going away. You are upset. When you are upset, you are focused. A strong emotion lingers right at the surface, refusing to sink away. I look at you and you are sharp. The skin around your eyes is tighter as if you had put on a mask. There is something in your eyes that is not leaving. I feel like I've talked-back to my mother. I sit up and close my book and say that I can look around for some coffee.

Oh wonderful, you say in a friendlier tone, but not without snark. I get up and walk to the faucet. I fill up the quick boil kettle, then grab one of your mugs from the table.

Make sure it's strong. I want it tough.

I take a deep breath.

Put some hair on your chest, I say and you laugh.

Your head is down again and you laugh into the table.

I spoon the instant coffee grounds into the mug as the water starts to boil. I pour the water in. The mouth of the mug fills with steam and the flat black liquid rises in it. I put the coffee down in front of you and you say oh my, you're hired.

I sit back down and watch as you purse your lips and lower them down to meet the cup. You chuckle to yourself. I relax, but am still annoyed. You sip the coffee and go Ah, now that's nice. You smack your lips and wink: But it needs a little sugar.

I don't know where the sugar is.

That's ok. I got it here.

You lift the lid of a small jar in front of you. Your tongue is out, carefully bringing the spoon full of sugar to the cup. You do this three times, then take a sip.

A little more, I think, and you go for two more spoonfuls. You know, my father used to say that sugar would give you pinworms. What's a pinworm? I still have no idea.

You are just talking to yourself. I sit there and refuse to respond—you are just talking to yourself.

You lean forward and take a loud sip.

Just right, you say. Nice and sweet.

You take three more sips, muttering things like Wonderful! and Delicious! into the cup. Eventually you tire again, put the mug down and slide it away from you. You lower your head to the table and settle in there. I watch as some strands of hair follow you down, falling gently into the dark of your coffee. You do not notice and I do not say anything.

You write notes to yourself. Like leaves, they curl at their corners over time and are brittle by the time I pick them up from the table and read them.

Your hair is in your breakfast. Breakfast is not for sleeping thru.

I find them on yellow sticky notes, on the backs of catalogues, scraps of notebook paper, junk mail, opened envelopes all scattered about the kitchen table. Some are older, the handwriting neat and slanted, in cursive.

Doctor's Appointment. Thursday 10:30

Or,

More fruit. Less sugar and cheese. Can not eat protein. Soup ok.

On most of them, the writing is shaky and disproportionate. The letters start out large and become cramped and fall away as they run out of room before meeting the end of the paper. They are hard to read. You can barely read them too. You pick up a scrap of paper and squint at it. You hold it in front of you and smirk, then hand it to me.

What does this say?

I take it and make it out. It says: Twin-steepled, stapled to rock.

You repeat it to yourself. Twin-steepled, stapled to rock.

I think that's your poem, I say.

My poem?

Yes. That's what you had told me before.

You laugh and your eyes are small and bright.

My poem. You shrug. I guess I'll take your word for it.

It's a good line.

Oh, well thank you. I think it's about the town, you say gesturing out the window.

There are the two steeples that stick up from the

cluster of the village: one for the Congregational Church and the other for the Unitarian Church. The water turns white as it breaks against the rocky neck below these steeples—we can see them from your window because it is winter and the leaves on the trees are down.

I think I have lived here my whole life, you say.

Yes, I think that's true.

You put your head down and I place the note back on your side of the table so you will find it again.

Later, you lift your head and look out the window. The sun reflects off the layer of snow covering the yard and you squint out through the glass. You turn to me and smirk like you did before and say, Twin-steepled, stapled to rock...

I nod and you kind of shrug and say, It's a poem I wrote, I think, a long time ago.

It's a good line, I say.

It is about the town, and you gesture out the window, but I do not look. I think I have lived here my whole life, you say.

Unless you choose to move somewhere else, I point out.

You like the thought.

Oh yes, that would be something. You smile and think for a moment: I could move to Paris.

Oui oui, I say and you coo warmly as you close your eyes. Or maybe Alaska? I propose. I don't know what made that come to mind but it makes you chuckle.

I do love the cold.

Alright pack your bags then. Alaska it is.

Oh you're a riot. You're too much, you say.

You shake your head, Alaska, you repeat, low and into the table and I imagine you there. I have never been to Alaska so the town I put you in is similar to your town here with its cramped roads congested by accumulated snow. I see you there in your black coat, lumbering up the road. You are all shoulders amongst the snow drifts and piles. You have no face. Your hood swallows your head. People watch you from a distance, from their warmth. Their breaths flowering on the window panes in front of them. You come in from the wild like a bear and they say look who's come to town. And I am there with you too. I can not see you without being there. I follow you, lagging behind like I'm your cub. People watch us and they say look who's come to town.

You are sleeping when I find a note on the table that says you were married forty years ago today.

You ask me to tell you about myself. I don't want to. I shrug. I don't know what to say.

Tell you about myself?

You roll your eyes: Of course! It's not every day that you get such an interesting person visiting you in your kitchen. Where are you from?

I'm from California.

Goodness, and you make a show of slumping your shoulders. California sure is a big place.

Yes. I grew up in San Diego.

And pretend I know nothing about San Diego— where is San Diego in California?

Southern California. As far south as you can go before you're in Mexico.

So interesting. What was that like? You sit up to explain. See I'm a New Englander and Southern California and Mexico all sound very far off and exotic to someone like me.

Yes. It is very different than here. I gesture out the window at the panorama of whites and blues and grays beyond the glass. It doesn't snow in San Diego.

No snow really?

Really.

Oh my, I don't know if I could do that! You touch your chest and say proudly that you are a cold weather girl.

Yes, I know. You wilt in the heat.

You laugh, eyes closed. Have I said that before?

Yes.

I think I met my husband in the cold. We were skiing. He was a city boy and I was a country girl. Yes...we were skiing, I'm sure, in New Hampshire or Vermont, I think.

Yes.

I just love the snow. You look out the window. I'm

a cold-weather girl.

Yes.

I wilt in the heat. Have I said that before?

Yes.

And what about you? Do you like the snow?

Yes, but then I think about it. I like days when it snows but I don't like living in the snow so much, especially when the winter is long and the snow becomes old and dirty like it is now.

You nod and I can tell that you like the elaboration and nuance of my previous statement.

You have to be tough on the winter, you say. Can't let it be the boss. If it's tough on you, then you have to be tough right back.

I suppose that's one way to do it. I guess I'm not New England tough.

You sit up. No?

No.

What kind of tough are you then?

I shrug.

I-da-ho, you chuckle. I suppose it's a strange question: What kind of tough are you?

Your head drops a little and you close your eyes. There is a pause while you take a breath and sigh.

And remind me where you are from again? I'm sure you've told me this before—

I'm from California.

And pretend I know nothing about California... does it get cold like it does here?

In some parts of California it does, but the part I'm from doesn't. It is always very warm. Always seventy degrees and sunny.

Sounds like vacation! But how on earth did you get out here?

To Massachusetts?

Yes, and you start high with your yes and slide down it, each s a drop in tone as you hold it out. Yessss... you say.

I drove my car.

Well, that's quite a trip.

Yeah, it took awhile.

Was it for school?

No. I just decided to move out here.

Oh my goodness! Just like that? You lift up your hand and give it a flick like your dusting a shelf. Just like that, you move?

Well, not just like that.

You nod for me to go on.

No, I thought about it for a while.

And what made you choose to move here? You tap the table with the ends of your fingers. What made you choose here out of all the places in the country?

I don't know.

You laugh. Your eyes are on me, narrowed. You shrug and your voice goes high.

I don't know, you say and laugh again.

Yeah, I don't know.

I-da-ho, *Alaska*, you say and laugh again.

I just wanted to move, I say. Wanted something different.

You nod and wipe your nose with your finger. You close your eyes. You are thinking.

I've never moved. I've lived in this house my whole life, you say.

I know, I say.

You laugh: Have I said that before?

·Ọ·　　　·Ọ·　　　·Ọ·

First, it is the comb.

I unzip your purse and find it—I hand you the comb.

You're wonderful, you say, taking it in your hand. You cock your head so your hair falls over your right shoulder and you feed in its teeth. The comb bites your hair, I hear some strands snap. Knots snag the teeth and you let out an oomf, pull the comb back and try again until it breaks through.

I have seen you take the comb handle with both hands against a burl of hair.

After you finish, you clean the comb's teeth. You floss a tangled nest of silver hair from between its prongs and let the mess fall from your hand. The hair catches the light as it falls—a brief leaf in slow descent. I watch as the hair misses the trash can and goes to the floor, disappearing into the complicated design of the rug.

You hand the comb back to me and I put it back in your purse.

We move on to the lipstick.

I hand you the lipstick before you even ask for it—I know it comes after the comb. You take it and your eyes are wide and smiling at me, how wonderful it is that I know what comes next. You're hired, you say taking the lipstick. It is hard for you to uncap the tube—your hand gives you trouble often, it is hard for you to grip such a small thing. I offer to help but you say no, no and put the tube in your mouth. You bite it and pull with your teeth and the cap does not give and I grimace looking at you, your face pinched and lopsided as you sink your teeth into the plastic tube and pull until finally the cap pops off. Your whole body jumps back from the release, then you chuckle as you spit the cap out into your open hand. You apply the lipstick to your lips.

I'm pretty old fashioned, you say.

Oh?

Oh yes, I don't go out without putting this stuff on.

Oh, I see.

Do the girls now use lipstick?

I think they still do.

Really? You say, finishing up and capping the tube. Well I don't go anywhere without putting it on.

I hand you a napkin and you round your lips and mouth the fold of it, leaving a red mark.

Ok, ready to get going? I ask, opening the purse for you to drop the lipstick in.

Almost, you say and you stand up. I must visit the ladies' room.

Sounds good. You hit the head and then we'll head out.

You laugh at this and repeat *hit the head and head out* under your breath as you shuffle out of the room. You love that pun. It reminds you of your husband taking you sailing when you were both young and dating and how, eventually, both of your children learned to sail in the town harbor. Your summers would be spent at the yacht club, attending events, sitting out on the deck, socialising and watching the boats go out. Old friends of yours we meet in town often lean over to me and say watch out for this one, wagging their finger at you, she was infamous for the parties she'd throw back in the day. Wild times with her, and you shake your head, smiling.

I suppose I was a little wild back then. But I've settled down, and you wink at me.

You close the door to the bathroom and I pick up

your heavy winter coat. I hold onto the purse and throw the jacket over my arm. I stand in your kitchen and wait. I look out the window and it is a flat winter's day. Not much to see. I am tired of the snow. I check the time and we'll be fine. Normally, I try to leave earlier so we can get a bit of a walk in but it is too cold out and the parking is a little tougher because there are snowbanks lining the sidewalk, piling onto the road. The streets are so small in town that any snow chokes the flow of traffic, reducing two lanes to one and pushing people out into the streets.

We won't walk far, if we walk at all, and you'll be happy about that. You'll say park as close as you can to the restaurant, I don't feel like walking today, and I'll say okay and that will be the end of it. I look at my hands and make sure I have everything you need while I wait: I have your bag and coat, I have my backpack and I pat my pockets, yes, I got my car keys and wallet. I have already put the walker in the back seat of my car. Even if you aren't walking far it is good for you to use it.

I hear the flush of the toilet and the faucet run. You open the door and I meet you there at the end of the hall with your winter coat open for you to put on. You look at it and then look past me to try and see the chair with your other coats on it. I say it is very, very cold out, giving the coat a little flick to get your attention back to it. You nod and turn so I can work your arms through and over your shoulders. It is easier because you are standing.

Does this have a hood? you ask.

Yes.

Excellent, you say and we start down the hallway to the front door.

Outside, it is bitter and cold. I help you out the front door and you shudder in the wind.

Does this coat have a hood? you ask again as I take

your hand. I don't answer, just throw the hood up over your head. It drops over your face and you laugh, lifting it up with your hand so you can see.

A walkway is already dugout in the snow leading from the front door to the driveway. We walk slow, taking small steps, careful not to slip. You grip my hand hard. You stop and look up.

Is that your car?

There she is.

I have to step into a snow pile to open the door for you. Snow gets into my shoes. You grip the door and lift your foot into the car. The coat is bulky, the hood slips again over your eyes. You keep on, hunched and grunting your way into the car. I hold the door still as you negotiate your way into your seat, falling into place.

Very smooth, I say and place the purse at your feet. I reach over you and buckle you up and you are already tired. Your eyes are closed and your head is back. Your lips are pinched tight as you breathe through your nose.

Ok, I say and close the door. I hurry around and get into the car. I start it and the vents on the dashboard growl. The heat will kick in soon, I say rubbing my hands together. I look over to you and you are still slumped in your chair, the coat seems to be growing over you in real time. Your eyes are narrowed, going over something. I blow onto my hands and put the car in reverse.

What happened there? you ask and I look over and you are pointing to the broken windshield. I had forgotten about it and grown used to it, the large crack stretching across the glass. I look at it and remember and my face gets hot. I turn away from you and put the car in reverse.

It's nothing I say, quickly. I don't want to talk about it.

Is it ok?

It's just a crack.

I look over my shoulder and start to back up. The tires spin for a moment and I think *come on* before the treads grip and we jolt back out of the driveway.

But what happened? you ask. I can see you're not taking your eyes off the windshield. You're slumped in your chair, cowering from the glass like you're afraid it will shatter at any moment. Johnny Cash starts to sing but you don't notice. You normally ask me who is singing, if this is Johnny Cash, but you don't because your eyes are stuck on the crack. You can't forget it.

A rock hit it, I say.

I don't look over at you. I want you to drop it but you don't. My answer doesn't stick.

What happened? you ask again and I say again: a rock hit it.

Has it always been there?

No, I say, but it's fine.

You do not believe me and we drive into town.

III.

Birds of Massachusetts

YOUR NEIGHBOR WORKS on the other side of the low stone wall. She is on her knees and I see the spade in her gloved hand as she lifts it up and drives it down into her flower bed. Her dog trots around her, sniffing the tree trunks and plants, sitting briefly before getting up again and nosing about in a bush. I can see its tongue, the white of its stomach, the white of its tail, hair hanging long and the neighbor drives the spade down.

I rest my elbow on the table and watch her with no particular interest other than that she is out there, beyond the kitchen window, and I can see her and watch her without being watched. The sun bakes the pane. Its heat palms my face and the neighbor drives the spade down. She is bringing up weeds and old root and turning the soil—finally winter is over. It has taken most of the spring with it but the cold is gone now.

Outside the window are birds. Lint breasted sparrows scurry in the hedge, burrowing about in its twig. They flit from the hedge to the feeder hanging from the porch. They take a seed, then arc back to the hedge. They throw a feather-fit in the stone water of the bath, ruffling their feathers up, puffing out their dusty breasts. They fall to the ground. I lose them there, in the tall grass, moving about with their beaks down looking for grub.

Out in the orchard behind the garden, crows stalk. Four of them loiter like construction workers. I look to you and you are sleeping and I smile at the thought of shouting out, screaming, there's a murder in the garden! You would wake quick and get up quick forgetting your legs are bad, forgetting that you're old and supposed to move slow, and you'd be razzled and young with your cheek still flat and pressed from the table. You'd go to the window and go where? what? how? not understanding and I'd smirk. I'd be all coy over here in my chair and clarify: *a murder of crows*. You would love that. You would shake your head, going back to your chair, and repeat *a murder of crows* under your breath, sitting down and laughing, *a murder of crows*.

The neighbor's dog jumps over the wall into your yard. It starts to run and bark as if it's chasing something and the neighbor stands up and calls out its name. The dog continues on across the yard towards the house. The birds scatter. The neighbor follows it over the stone wall into your yard, calling out the dog's name, clapping and slapping her thigh, calling out its name again and again. The dog trots below the kitchen window, right under us. I lean forward in my chair so to see the dog sniffing the hedge there. The bush shivers with the small birds. The neighbor walks up and grabs the dog by the collar. She mutters something, something like dang dog, don't you know your own name when it's called, dang dog. The dog hangs its tongue and whines and she yanks it back. The dog yelps, then bounds back across the yard. The neighbor glances up towards us in the kitchen window, mouths *sorry*, and waves. I sit up, surprised, and look over to you. You are asleep, so I hold up my hand and wave in your stead. I don't know if she can see me, but I hold up my hand as if to say it's ok, as if this was my house.

I think about how your husband left this morning. You didn't say goodbye when he disappeared down the steps to the garage. Your head was down on the table. You were trying to get comfortable and sleep but the room was so warm. Then the garage door below us started to open and you sat up at the familiar sound. You rubbed your eyes, then grabbed the edge of the table and scooted yourself in the chair so you could better see the driveway as your husband backed the car out of the garage. I watched too and couldn't help but smile at how an old man backed out of his garage, how the car moved in inches, how the brake lights flickered, off and on off and on, then finally, the slow crank of the tires as they straightened out before pulling up the driveway.

You sat up in your chair as the long stroke of the Oldsmobile turned out onto the road and into your vision. Your husband stuck his arm out of the car window and started to wave, knowing you were watching. He waved with his whole arm, up and down, and you stood up and waved too. You planted one hand on the table for balance and leaned forward, waving to him.

Can he see me? you asked.

Yes, I said, he knows you are here, that's why he's waving.

You continued to wave, still standing—your hand back and forth at the wrist. He kept waving too. His arm moved slow like a gull's wing.

Can he see me?

He knows you are waving.

You didn't sit down until he pulled his arm in and the car turned out of sight. You then lowered yourself back into your chair, closing your eyes and biting your bottom lip. You put your head down and said, Oh, he's a good husband, into the table.

The neighbor and dog are back on their side of the wall.

You flinch in your sleep and the table shifts. There are a variety of birds in the hedge below your window. Some are the same, small black and white bulbs of body and feather that trade branches outside of my basement window. I go to the shelf in your hallway and pick a book I have seen there before—the spine is blue with white lettering, titled *The Birds of Massachusetts*. I go back to the kitchen and match the birds below to their glossy images on the page. They are the Black-Capped Chickadees, from the tit family, who are known for their memory and their courage around humans. I open up a section of the window to hear their chitter through the screen. A breeze comes in and eddys around the room.

Oh wonderful, you coo from your dreams, feeling the air move around you. I lean towards the window to hear the birds' songs. The sounds are constant and light: when one bird rests for a breath another sings.

And there is a Tufted Titmouse, its punkish plume and awkward lift of its body gawky and noticeable amongst the others. I watch it as it eyes the feeder from a bush along the garden fence. It is tentative, working up the courage to approach the feeder and the other birds. Finally it lifts off, arcs and collides with the perch, nearly slipping from it as it swings, and the chickadees scatter and regroup elsewhere. The titmouse hastily takes a seed and bounds away, wanting to bury its head in its breast. I could not hear its song. It says in the book that often they are shy, and when they whistle, they whistle a peter-peter-peter.

I look up from the book to check on you and your head is up.

You are smiling at me.

What is it that you got there?

I lift up the book and show you the cover.

A book, I say.

Oh, is that what those are...I had no idea. You laugh at your joke, then nod. Will you read some to me?

Well, it's mostly pictures of birds with some information under them.

Oh my—the pitch of your voice rises—sounds interesting.

I shrug, lean forward over the book, flip to a random page and read aloud the bullet points below the photograph.

I tell you that a Rock Pigeon is a bird of Massachusetts and its young have little lustre in their feathers. I tell you that the birds are typically monogamous and have up to two squabs in their brood and that makes you laugh because it is like you: typically monogamous with two birds hatched in your brood. And did you know that the Rock Pigeon can not dip its beak and drink water continuously, but has to tilt up its head to swallow? And that is like you too, your slow hand reaching across the table for that glass of water, pulling it towards you taking a deep breath and trying to meet it halfway with your lips before you jerk the glass up and your head is back and the water charges your mouth drowning you and then you go ahhhh setting the glass down refreshed and relieved that you do not have to drink again for at least a little while.

Fascinating, you say. Will you read me another?

I nod, sure, and flip to another page that says that seagulls are also birds and also of Massachusetts. It says that they live long lives and some have even been recorded to have lived for as long as forty-nine years. It says that seagulls are very intelligent birds with orange beaks that they use as tools for dropping breadcrumbs in water to bait fish and some gulls have even been seen diving onto the backs of whales to pick and feed at their flesh. This makes you proud when I read you this, so proud you pick up your head and tell me to read it again and read it slow. I do and you look out to the slice of ocean water above the trees full of leaves as you listen and it makes you proud to think that everyone in Massachusetts, even the seagulls, are hunters of whales.

You peel back your lips and squint your eyes and I see the gull in you. You are of Massachusetts. You have lived a long life here and you have been built to weather any weather. You have long teeth to grind down during the long New England winters that turn into muddy and short springs.

You told me that your husband went on a few dates with Sylvia Plath before he met you. He said she was too sensitive, but you, stubborn and low to the ground with wide shoulders and wide hips, were a perfect ballast for his ship.

You tell me this story all the time and I think it comes to you because when you see me you think the same thing: *too sensitive* ; or, *not built to last*; or, *he would not eat the flesh of a whale in order to survive.*

When I walk in and sit across from you or take your hand and stand next to you, it is your presence that dominates and fills the room. I am small compared to you and overwhelmed. I'm not exciting, or tough. I'm not a seagull and I can tell it disappoints you. I bore you and maybe that's why you sleep. Choosing dreams to me, memories to the reality in front of you. I know I don't carry on conversations very well—I answer one of your questions with one word or two, and you look at me in expectation, waiting for me to say more. You nod your head and turn your hand over in the air as if to say: *Go on... Elaborate...*

In my silence, you wait and think you might as well put the ol' head down. I have been with you long enough that when I walk in and you see me, without knowing or remembering why, you think might as well put the ol' head down.

Sometimes I think your disease is getting worse and it's my fault. Maybe if I was more of a talker, if I spoke to you more I could somehow make your memory sharper, your mind more active and more energized throughout the morning I spend with you. I can do that, I should be doing that—though I am so skeptical of these words that come from my mouth, that repeat and repeat and repeat themselves.

I already know the stories you tell. I have asked you questions and I know your answers. I have been with you through seasons. Days have passed over us, between us. The table and all of its clutter never changes. You've told me the story about you and your sister going into the city with your grandfather and you've told me how you had a dog that would track mud in the house after playing in the rain and how your father and your husband were both in the military and how you sailed at the yacht club and went to parties and church in town. You've told me about this town, how you love this town. You wrote a poem about it: *Twin-steepled, stapled to rock.*

There is nothing new. Nothing progresses in our days. How can it when the moment I walk out the front door you forget me?

I am like a bird in your home. My heart beats in my eyes, looking this way and that, checking my head this way and that. I flit and freeze. I walk with high knees and reaching toes. I stalk around and make my feet soft when I'm in your house. I speak low. I keep my eyes low. I go to the bathroom and close the door softly. I turn the faucet on low and wash my hands. I grimace as I flush the toilet, my thoughts begging the water shhhh as it runs. I sit still in my chair, perched on this perch. I'm afraid to chitter or trill, to peter-peter-peter. I'm afraid that if I give you a fright while you're sleeping, you'll jump up and scream. You'll see me and not remember who I am and come at me with the bristle-side of a broom, sweeping me towards the nearest open window as I flutter my wings and bang against the walls and ceiling trying to convince you that it is okay, I am supposed to be here. I am a bird of Massachusetts! I am a bird of Massachusetts! I'd sing.

·ỗ·   ·ỗ·   ·ỗ·

It is my day off and I have nothing to do. The woods are loud with the activity of new life as I walk up the long driveway to the barn to poke around the piles of junk that have accumulated there over the years. Countless bed frames, dressers and cabinets, rusted bicycles, an old canoe hanging from the rafters, unused shop tools, sagging boxes full of clothes and books and whatever. It is just a storehouse of junk. It feels like the whole building with everything in it could fall back off its stilts into the woods at any moment and no one would care.

I pick through the barn, looking for nothing, enjoying its cool. I lift up a blue tarp and find a pile of cinder blocks and wood boards tucked underneath it. The wood seems to be in better condition than most things here and I think that maybe I could use both the boards and blocks to build a bookshelf for my room. My books are still stacked in the same columns and piles I put them in when I first moved into my basement room. The stacks have only gotten more and more disorganized since then, lopsided and leaning, with more and more books balanced on their tops.

I went to the hardware store when I first moved to buy some wood and screws to build a bookshelf myself. It was something I had always wanted to do—to build a simple thing quickly and use immediately. A house for my books. I had sketched out a design with a list of needed supplies on a piece of paper and I spent an hour in the store figuring out the type of wood I wanted, the type of varnish and how many boards I needed. I went up to the cash register with all of my wood boards piled up and my wallet in my hand and then found out as the tags were scanned that wood was a lot more expensive than

I realized. I flinched when the cashier said the total out loud, but I couldn't bring myself to say anything. I didn't want to spend that much money. I couldn't afford it, but I handed over my card anyway and turned hot and red as she charged it. I took the wood back to my car and sat in the parking lot, looking over the receipt, furious with myself, swearing at myself, telling myself that I shouldn't have paid that much for wood. I can just find wood on the street, at the dump or around the property. I didn't need to waste money on something I could scrounge together.

Finally, I went back in the store, embarrassed and angry with myself, and returned the wood I had bought ten minutes before.

That was sometime last summer and the shelf has gone unbuilt. So seeing the cinder blocks stacked there next to the wooden boards in the back of the barn, the idea to just stretch the wooden boards between two columns of cinder block to make myself a bookshelf comes to me fully formed as it had been gestating in my head for the past year.

I choose three two-by-fours in good condition and six cinder blocks and load them into a wheelbarrow. I roll the load out of the barn and instead of taking the driveway down the hill to my basement room, I turn into the woods and take the long way, down the overgrown fire road that empties out onto the street a block away. I take the fire road because I don't want to run into one of the tenants or Gus. I know they'll see me and wonder what I'm up to. Gus will certainly ask what're ya doing kid? Or, where'd ya get that wood and those cinder blocks kid? And I'm sure it's fine that I'm using the wood and cinder blocks, but I just don't want him, or anyone else, to ask me about what I'm doing. I don't want to explain what I'm going to do with the wood and cinder blocks, and if I run into Gus, he'd probably say something like well, I wouldn't do it that way, and then he'd offer up some advice or worse, his help, and I'd have to say no thanks, not trying to be rude or anything, I just want to do this on my own. I just want to build this bookshelf from scratch, my way, quickly and quietly, on my own, and when it's done it will be done as if it was always there, in my room, done.

It is hard pushing the wheelbarrow down the dirt road. The ground is uneven and steep. I almost lose the load trying to keep up with it, digging my heels into the ground to try and slow the wheelbarrow's speed down the hill. It tips aggressively and I set it down fast to prevent it from falling over. This happens a couple of times. I finally get to the road and turn towards the house. I stick to the side of it—there's no sidewalk. My arms are tired, strained at the elbows. The front wheel might be a little flat too. A car drives by and I keep my head down—I'm sure the driver looks at me as they pass, trying to figure out what I'm doing walking a wheelbarrow full of wood and cinder blocks up a residential road. Probably up to something. I keep my head down. I keep walking and turn up the driveway to my house. The neighbor sees me as he gets out of his car and I smile and quickly navigate the wheelbarrow up to the basement door. I set down the load and catch my breath before propping the door open with a cement block and carrying the boards into my room. I set the wood in a pile and bring in each cinder block one at a time. I move the books from the wall and start assembling the shelf. I place two of the cinder blocks on the floor first, then lay the first board across them. It fits perfectly between my desk below the window and the couch. I'll be able to get to a book when I write at my desk or when I am relaxing on the couch. I put the next two cinder blocks in position and lay the next board across them. Within minutes, the shelf is complete. I do it almost too quickly—it took longer to load and unload the wheelbarrow than to build this thing. But I don't mind. It is done.

I get a beer from my fridge and sit down to start organizing my books, putting them in piles according to their authors' last name. I occasionally flip through a book I had forgotten about or had not read in a long time. I read a couple of lines here and there, leafing through its pages, remembering where I was when I came to own it. My father gave me this one, or I bought this one in New Mexico driving across the country, or I bought this one when I drove up to Portland. I take stock of each book and put them in their respective order. I've nearly gone through all of them when I find the copy of *Moby Dick* I had tried to read so many times before. Call me Ishmael— that is how it goes. The first line. I turn the book over in my hands. Call me Ishmael. The book is compact with its spine ends worn white by the shelf and the covers' corners are starting to split. I picked it up from a 50 cent bin in San Francisco. I explored the city with it in my pocket. I don't remember anything about that day, except buying the book and putting it in my pocket. I really do need to read this book. I'm embarrassed I haven't yet, thinking about all the times I've sat down and tried to tackle it, only to get skin deep. Call me Ishmael. How great it would be to really read and understand this book; how great it would be to read it in one great burst of energy, in one go from morning into the night. One long day. Call me Ishmael. Yes. *Moby Dick* would be my book and I'd do nothing but sing its praises. I'd go to arms with any and every detractor I cross. People would moan that it's too long and too boring and I'd smile as they'd say this, knowing that they are wrong, so completely wrong. I'd find it on the shelf of every bookstore I visit and say there is *Moby Dick* by

Herman Melville. I have read that book. I know that book.

I get up and set the book on my desk. I'll bring it along with me when I see you tomorrow. You'll ask me to read something, something *interesting*, you'll say and I'll say oh I got just the thing, pulling the book out of my bag, opening to its first page. Call me Ishmael, I'll say and you will coo with pleasure. Such a wonderful start, what an opening line! and maybe I'll read the whole thing to you right there in your kitchen! That's the way to do it. Each day I'll come in and you, knowing exactly who I am, would say read me that book you've been reading, it's so *interesting*, and I'll happily take it out, cough to clear my throat, and continue on where we had left off the previous day. Call me Ishmael and on and on, following the lines on, knowing what to say because here are the words written out for me and I'll say them and you'll react—you will grin with pleasure or jump in fright or ask me to repeat a line I had just read because it was such a wonderful line and I'll oblige: Call me Ishmael, I'll say and you'll nod, that's the one, what an *interesting* line, and I'll feel good because I am interacting with you. We'll be sharing this tangible thing. This long and beautiful book, whole and complete, will be between us.

I step back to admire how my room has come together. The wall there with its high window letting in light over my bed; the chair there pushed into the spartan desk with its notebooks full of my scribblings; and now the bookshelf there, heavy with books. The space is uncluttered and simple. It is in the ground. It feels like it could be mine.

I sneeze and you are up.

You pull your head up as if coming up from water, gasping I'm up I'm up.

You hold your head back, point your nose towards the ceiling to fight the weight of your head. It will just fall back down if you don't, if you let it.

You laugh. Jesus, you say.

I sit up in my chair. What about him? I ask and you laugh.

You lower your head and laugh again. Your eyes are still closed. You wipe your chin with the back of your hand.

Jesus, isn't it awful how tired I am?

I nod and look up at the clock.

So what is the plan? you ask.

You have still not opened your eyes. You lean forward in your chair.

Just our typical day. We'll hang out here for a bit and then go into town.

And what will we do in town?

We're going to lunch remember?

The word slips out and I feel guilty—I try not to say *remember*. I know it's not helpful or useful and I imagine it's frustrating for you because you do not remember. I lean towards you to apologize, as if to show you with my body that I am sorry, but you do not see. Your eyes are closed.

Oh, no, I do not remember, but how exciting! you say.

Yes, it's very exciting. I put on a smile.

You lower your head onto the table. All I can see is the top of your head and the blue line of skin from which your hair grows.

I'm just going to put my head down for a minute and then we will go, ok?

Ok.

I look out the kitchen window and there is the garden. The soil is black from yesterday's rain, but nothing was planted so nothing is growing. There are the trees, light-leafed and white-barked, lining the yard by the low stone wall. Your neighbor is not there this morning. Above their green is a piece of ocean, flat and without sound, just like the sky.

I open up one of the windows and a breeze sifts through the screen into the kitchen, carrying the cool of the water. It gets so stuffy in your house. The air in here is so stale from the coughing heaters and spitting furnaces running all winter and too far into spring. I stand up from the table and open the sliding glass door that leads out onto the porch.

Let's get some fresh air in here, I say.

You mumble into the table.

The wind flows up the hill into the room and it feels like the whole house starts to breathe. I hear your snore from the kitchen—it is shyer now, like a whistle. I go into the hallway and open the front door to give the air direction, so it flows out and through rather than piling up with nowhere to go.

I walk back up the long hallway. I can hear the birds chittering outside. I can hear the leaves. I look at the pictures of you on the wall. You grew up in this house. You have never lived anywhere else. There you are with your sister in the yard. There you are in a christening gown in your mother's arms. You got your nose from her. You got your eyes from your father—there you are on a bike with him standing behind you keeping your balance with a light, steadying hand. Two sets of the same eyes: small and sharp, coming out from heavy brows. Here you are with your husband, sitting in the living room I was in just moments ago, holding your newborn. Here you are with two young sons. Here you are on the porch in sunglasses. Here you are, suddenly older now, touching the petals of a sunflower in your garden. I walk up the hallway, studying pictures I have walked past countless times and feel a fresh breeze push past me—I am finding the life in this house. Not giving it a new one, no, but picking it up like it's an old book and fanning out its pages so it can breathe. Let this book breathe. I go back into the kitchen. Your face is still down. You are mumbling. I can't hear what you're saying but I smile. Right now, today, it is endearing—how you sleep with your head on the table like that; how you sleep-talk nonsense; how you wake and fall asleep again and again, saying I'll be up soon, five more minutes.

The life in this house is your life. This is so clear to me right now, sitting down at the table across from you, that I grin, amazed that it has taken me so long to realize such a thing. I have been selfish with my time here. I have worried so much about myself, sitting there across the table from you, that I have not opened myself up to being here in this home. I scan back through our days together and I realize that I have not been here with you. I have not sat down in this room without thinking I shouldn't be here, some part of me wishing I was gone.

I take out my copy of *Moby Dick* . I'll start reading this, I think, and you will wake and see me here, reading, and ask: What are you reading? Sounds interesting, will you read me some?

I scoot my chair back from the table so I can cross my legs. The chair cackles. I open the book and read its first line.

Call me Ishmael.

That's how it begins. Like so many things, it begins and then it goes on. Feeling its pages on my fingers: brown and soft—there is dust on the paper.

I look up from the book—you are snoring now. Your back lifts and your lips whinney with the heavy exhale. Deep in sleep.

It is such a beautiful day and it feels even more beautiful and rare thinking about how long winter had been. I want to get in my car, roll down the windows, and explore, pulling down thin paths off main roads to hidden coves, fruiting orchards, and unkept meadows. I want to drive to the end of Granite Pier and watch the waves crash into the rock.

An itch comes over me and the room begins to feel hot. Just like that, I don't want to sit anymore. I want to go to all these places, but I can not. You are here. I can not just get up and go. I'd have to wait for you to wake up, to comb your hair, to put on your coat, to walk down the hallway, to get in the car. You'll ask where we are going. Where are you taking me? and I'll have to answer, to explain to you that I just want to drive, to try something different today, to park on the side of the road and walk into the woods. It is now all-of-a-sudden hard to breathe here in your kitchen. You are here. In this place, for these mornings, we are tied and tethered to each other.

I try to go back to the book but it is impossible to read now. It feels so thick and distant—like dropping pebbles into black water, trying to follow them down. Call me Ishmael. A period. The end of a sentence. A pebble from my hand: it drops, plops, jags in the syrup and is gone. I drop another—the words on the page fall from me. Call me Ishmael—they pass through the water's murk, blinking with turning light, getting deeper and then gone.

Call me Ishmael, for it is back to the beginning.

With you—it is always back to the beginning.

Out the window: the untethered ocean. It goes on

and on.

I close the book and flip the pages along my thumb. Covered in words that go deeper and deeper on each sheet, front and back and such small lettering with so little paragraph breaks and it all seems to me a hassle— diving in, holding my breath, getting doused, knowing it.

Somehow the air has changed. The house and you have not moved, but everything has shifted in my relation to it. What is wrong with me? It is like I am hungry, but nauseated by the very thought of food.

I sneeze again and you chuckle into the table. You lift your head up and I sneeze again.

Goodness, do you have a cold?

It's just allergies.

You smirk. If you're sick you can always take a day off. I think I'll be able to manage without you, you say.

It's just allergies.

You nod.

Why don't you read me something since you're sitting there. Read me something *interesting* from whatever you got there.

I look down at the book open in front of me.

Call me Ishmael—on and on it goes.

I look up at you. There are your blue eyes—it is impossible. I'm so afraid, I become indifferent. I close the book, hide it away in my backpack, and pick up an old copy of the town newspaper folded on the table. It is dated a week ago. I scan the front page looking for something easy to read to you. I hear your chuckle through the paper.

How are the Sox doin? you call out in a Boston accent.

I fold the paper down so I can see you.

What?

You nod to the paper. How're the Sox?

Oh, well this is an old paper so I couldn't tell you exactly.

Oh, ok.

Your smile fades a bit. I lower the paper.

But I think they're doing pretty good. It's still early in the season, but they have a good team this year.

Oh, that's good to hear. I love the Red Sox...Have I told you how my grandfather would take my sister and I to Fenway all the time?

I nod. You'd take the train, right?

You bite your lip trying to remember. Your head bobs a little hanging over the table.

Yes. Oh it was quite the trip for a country girl like me. I remember looking out the window for the entire ride, watching the trees and marshes and big houses slowly becoming roads and apartment buildings.

I sit up in the chair and cross my arms. That must've been pretty exciting.

Of course, we were going to the big city!

Do you remember any of the players you saw? I ask.

You close your eyes and recite: DiMaggio, Pesky, Williams, Doerr...That's all I remember.

I laugh. That's pretty impressive

You open your eyes again. Ted Williams was my favorite. Such a handsome man, tall and thin, but strong. My sister and I loved Ted Williams.

You must've got some pretty good looks at him.

Of course! We're not going to go all the way into the city and sit in the nosebleeds.

I guess you're right.

We are both smiling. Again, your eyes close and you dip your face towards the table. Your whole body is forward. Your lips get small and you seem to be focused on something else, something right in front of you that I can not see.

How is he doing? You open your eyes and look at me. This season, I mean.

Who?

You laugh. Ted Williams, of course!

Oh. Well, he's dead now.

Oh really? and you chuckle, shaking your head. Well, I hope that doesn't affect his swing.

My legs are sore today. My eyes hurt too. I look out the window. The light is too bright and I close my eyes. I have a headache, or the seed of one, distant and pulsing, growing somewhere in my brain.

I look at the clock. It is finally time to go.

I call your name to wake you. It is time to get ready. It is time to go. You hear my voice and coo. The table shakes as your body flinches. You laugh and say oh, wonderful, but you do not lift your head.

I stand up to show you that I am getting up, that I am up and it is time to go. I call your name again. It is time to get ready. It is time to go. We are going to go into town to get some lunch. Aren't you hungry 'cause I'm *stahving*, I say and I say it with a thick accent that I know you get a kick out of. You snort again and sigh. Your cheek is glued to the table. Your shoulders shift as if to lift it free but they can't unstick it.

Stahving, you mumble.

I look out the window and rest my voice. It feels good to stand.

I say that out loud: It feels good to stand.

You don't respond.

It is getting towards noon. We should be going soon. We need to go so we can be back in time to meet your husband. We are supposed to go get lunch in town and be back here at 1:15 to meet him. He is running errands right now.

I call your name again. I look at the clock.

I call your name again, louder and shorter, trying to sound authoritative. You do not respond. I sigh and look at my hands and then suddenly you gasp and your head shoots into the air.

I am up. I am up, you say, your whole upper body emerging from the table as if it was a pool. You throw your head back and point your nose towards the ceiling to fight the weight of your head.

You laugh. Jesus, you say.

I look up at you and say, a bit coldly, Oh, you're up. Are you ready to go?

Oh? you say and look right at me. And where are we going?

Into town, to get some lunch.

Oh, excellent. I could go for some lunch. And where were we planning on going?

I walk out from behind my chair and pick up your purse from the floor.

Where do you want to go?

I get to choose?

Of course, you're the one in charge. I'm just following your lead.

You laugh: Oh you're wonderful. Do you have a girlfriend?

No.

Well let me know when you get one and I'll tell her how wonderful you are.

Okay, sounds like a plan.

I open the purse. Everything is there: your wallet, your glasses, your comb and lipstick.

Well, shall we get going?

You are still sitting. I'm standing at the end of the table, trying to show you that I am up, that we are leaving.

Oh yes, but where are we going?

We're going to lunch.

I know that, and you roll your eyes dramatically, but *where*?

Where do you want to go?

Your eyes widen and you look up at me. You know what? you say and I know exactly what you are going to say. I would love a delicious piece of roast beef, you say.

We can do that. We'll go to the House of Roast Beef.

Is there such a thing?

Of course, we go there all the time.

You laugh, your eyes close and your head starts to droop. I watch it and I want to catch it, pull you up by your shoulders, snap and clap in front of your face and shout wake up wake up stop falling asleep stop it it is time to go!

Oh, I would love a delicious piece of roast beef, you say before your head, at last, returns to the table. I shake my head and close your purse.

I'm going to get the car ready and when I come back we'll leave, ok?

You rub your cheek against the plastic dinner tray.

I walk into the hallway. I grab the walker propped up against the wall next to the bookshelf and I carry it down the two steps to the front door. I set the walker down on the front step and guide the glass door back over the frame so it does not slam shut. I walk across the front yard to my car in the upper driveway. I slide the walker into the backseat, then make sure the front seat is clean. I give it a couple of brushes with my hand and clear out the area where your feet will go.

I pull a knot of silver hair from the seat's headrest. I pinch it with two fingers and quickly drop it over the grass where it slowly floats down and disappears.

I crack the window on your side and roll down the window on mine to get some air circulating through the car before you get in. It is a hot day and my air conditioning does not work. You are always suggesting to me that I fix it when I tell you that it doesn't work.

I don't have the money, I say.

Well, I'll pay for it.

Ok, next time. But for now, I've got the window down for you.

Yes, and it's lovely, but you can't beat air conditioning.

I close the car door and hear laughter and splashes coming from the quarry at the bottom of the road. I walk across the yard and try to see through the trees to the pool of water. I had never seen people swimming there before. The swimmers' sounds mosey up and taunt me. I can't see them through the dense branches. I want to walk down and check it out, maybe dip my toes in to test out the water. I never have before. How have I been coming to your house for this long and have never been down to the quarry? I should go right now. A swim would be nice. I check the front door of the house—it is still open. I am always paranoid about that. If the door closes, I'm locked out. I worry that you wouldn't hear if I knocked to try and get back in. I'd be worried about making a scene, yelling your name, walking around your house, calling your name from the hedge below the kitchen window for your neighbors to hear. I can see you lifting your head up, looking around the kitchen, before glancing outside and finding me down below in the yard, desperately waving my arms. You'd laugh, lean forward and try to open a window but be unable to, you'd have to walk around the table to the sliding glass door and come out onto the porch and look down at me sweating and desperate below you.

Hell-o, you'd sing, how can I help you? not remembering who I am.

Are you ok? I'd ask and you'd laugh.

Oh you're sweet.

You'd have to walk yourself to the front door to let me in.

What if you fell?

I want to walk down to the quarry and jump in, but I can not. I can not leave you alone for too long. I already feel guilty for leaving you alone.

A car door closes and I make eye contact with your neighbor up the hill. I wave. They're getting something out of their trunk. They nod hello.

It is too nice out to go back inside. You do not know you're alone. You're fine. I'm sure you are still asleep.

I watch as a seagull glides out from beyond the trees. It arcs above the house without moving its wings. It doesn't float down to the porch railing but continues on, out past the yard up towards the point of the cape further on up the road.

A breeze sends the tree leaves into applause.

Your house sits back into the hill, looking out towards the ocean.

The whole scene reminds me of something you said on the first day I was with you. You were sitting there in your chair and I was sitting in mine across the table from you and there was a lull between us. I looked out the kitchen window—it was summer then, and it is nearly summer again now—and I said something about the view, saying something about how beautiful the view was here. You chuckled in your way that was new to me then and looked out the window.

Oh yes, you said, We call it the ever-changing picture.

At first, I thought that meant that the landscape had so many different faces and looks that the view would be drastically different from day to day, refusing to be still or repeat itself. I expected a similar kind of transformation each morning I walked through your front door. I wanted each interaction between us to be an event of discovery and progress that bonded us together, but after nearly a year of each day with you being the same, I can stand here and look out at the trees and water and yard and see the same thing I saw that first day and understand that *ever-changing* means slow. It means repetition with the subtlest alterations and grace notes and trills. This place is an old thing adjusting itself the tiniest amount each day, and you are the same. You have planted yourself here and you can look out your kitchen window at the yard and trees and ocean and nod because you understand how all of this has changed and stayed the same throughout your life.

But I should get back. I have been outside for awhile. I glance back up towards your neighbor but they are gone. I quickly check that the car is ready to go then head back inside.

I walk up the long hallway into the kitchen and you are in your chair like always but your head is gone and under the table.

I laugh and ask what are you doing?

You sit up at my voice and laugh at my laughter. You look up at me quizzically.

Where did it go? you ask.

Where did what go?

You gape in surprise, then thin your eyes as if I'm pulling your leg. You glance under the table again.

The dog that was just here, of course!

I shake my head. What dog?

The dog that was just here. I felt it brush against my leg. You didn't see it?

I shake my head.

What kind of dog was it?

I didn't see a dog.

You didn't?

I shake my head.

Maybe you were dreaming.

I was dreaming?

Maybe you were dreaming.

Oh my goodness. Dreaming—I must've been dreaming.

You were asleep.

It felt so real.

You laugh. You close your eyes and tell me how you felt the dog brush your leg under the table, making all this clatter. I could hear the ring of its collar, you say, its paws against the floor as it ran out into the other room. There was laughter in the other room—just around the corner—there was laughter out of sight but I could still hear it. The dog did too, it was running to it, making such a ruckus, bumping into the bureau there, making the china rattle. You pause. We were never allowed to have the dog in the house. It was too rowdy, it'd bump into everything and drove my mother crazy. Especially in winter, my father would let it in after trouncing around in the snow, tracking all of its wet and mud into the house. Drove my mother crazy, she'd yell at him and me and my sister would laugh. He did it just for a laugh! We loved the little pooch. Yes, in the other room too, we'd be sitting on the couch laughing and calling its name and it would jump up and lick our faces. It was one of those big hairy dogs that thought it was as small as a squirrel. What kind of dog was it? Oh, my memory is god awful...

Again you look up at me as if I knew the answer.

What kind of dog was it? you ask.

I don't know, I say.

You didn't see it? It ran just in there a moment ago, making all this noise.

I shake my head and shrug—it's all I can do.

You laugh and shrug too.

·ộ·   ·ộ·   ·ộ·

What's the weather like out there?

It is very pleasant, I say.

You stand up, steadying yourself by the table, and pick through a pile of coats and sweaters on a chair.

Well, let's bring along one of these fleeces. A good New Englander doesn't go anywhere without a layer.

You pick at them with two fingers, trying to lift one up by the sleeve to get a better look.

Here, I say. I put down your purse and pick up each fleece to show it to you.

How about this orange one?

Oh isn't that wild.

Or this green one?

You look at it and then look to the chair, narrowing your eyes to see the options I'm not showing you.

What happened to the blue one? There should be a blue one.

I don't know what happened to the blue one. It's been missing the past couple of days.

Really? and you do not believe me. Your eyes go to the chair again to make sure.

I hold up the orange and green fleeces.

I think these are your best options.

Your eyes go from the orange to the green to the chair.

What about that black one?

That black one is for winter. It's too heavy.

Oh no...the black one is the one I want.

I think you're going to be too hot in it.

I'll be fine, you say and reach for it yourself, picking at the limp sleeve, trying to pull the coat out from the bottom of the pile. I let you try, knowing you won't be able to—your whole right arm is pretty useless. You continue at it, shaking the coat's limp arm, with your other palm planted on the kitchen table for balance.

I put the fleeces down and pull the coat out from the pile.

You smile. Oh thank you, you're so helpful.

I pick up your purse and drape the coat over my arm.

Ok, it's time to go.

Yes, I'm *stahving*, you say in a Boston accent.

You laugh and I smile.

We walk out of the kitchen. You follow behind me as I walk down the hallway carrying your coat and purse. I get to the front door and look back to see you, going slow, your head down on your feet and your good hand dragging along the wall. You stop and call out to me.

You got my purse and everything?

You bet, I say.

You're wonderful.

You continue on down the hallway, towards the steps where I take your hand, open the front door and help you over the threshold.

What a beautiful day, you say. Nice and warm.

I nod. About time.

We cross the front lawn hand in hand.

Is this your car? you ask.

There she is.

I help you into the front seat. I open the door for you and you say oh, you're such a gentleman, and I say just doing my job. I steady the door as you put your weight onto it as you try and lift your foot up and into the front seat. You manage it, but get caught with your head ducked low so you won't bang your head. You laugh and huff, shifting the foot you have planted on the driveway, trying to figure out a way to get that leg to follow the other. I offer to take your other hand but you ignore it. You have one foot in and one foot out and your upper body is folded at your stomach to protect your head. You chirp in discomfort, your shoe scuffles against the loose gravel, and you just fall into the seat.

Very smooth, I say.

I place your purse between your feet. I put the coat in the back seat by your walker so you will forget about it when we get into town.

All settled?

Oh, yes.

I grab the seat belt and reach over you to buckle you in. I hold my breath. I hear the click of the buckle and straighten up.

Ok, I say and close the car door.

I pause for a moment before I get in the car, taking in the fine weather. A breeze runs through the trees, clapping the leaves against each other. There is no laughter coming up from the quarry—the swimmers have left. Your house lays back on its hill. It is low and set.

I get in the car and you are sinking into your seat, your eyes closed and head tilted to the air coming through the open window. I turn the car on and Johnny Cash's *American V: A Hundred Highways* starts to play as I back out of the driveway.

You sit up at his voice, turning towards me, blinking your eyes.

Is this Johnny Cash?

Yup.

You chuckle. Oh, wonderful, you say and start to sing along as we drive into town.

Acknowledgments

Small sections of this book were originally published by The Esthetic Apostle & Rantoul Magazine.

Deep appreciation to my friends who read early bits and drafts of this book and/or encouraged me in my writing over the years: Tai, Nate, Sam, Aaron, Steve, Victoria, Owen, Mark, Dave, Katherine, Trey, Jonathan, Grace, David L. & Tony Oh; the Point Loma boys always: Devin, Jarrod, Bryce, Daniel & Stevie; and all the people at Heirloom East Bay.

I am very grateful for the feedback and time given by my professors and classmates at SFSU, especially Paul Hoover, Maxine Chernoff, Michelle Carter, Truong Tran & Carolina De Robertis. Thanks to Fourteen Hills, especially Rachel Huefner & Aleesha Lange for their hard work bringing this thing together.

I'd like to thank my family: the Kennedys, Donworths & Barbarias.

You have shown, and continue to show me, how to live life well. I love you all very much.

Again, to Laura...and who could forget our Blue.

Steven Kennedy has an MFA from San Francisco State University. *Birds of Massachusetts* is his first novel.